Hide and Seek

If she didn't die today, she'd die tomorrow or the next day. There was no way to hide completely. And was that living? Was it enough to live for another day, always knowing that she was being hunted, being followed, being watched for the perfect moment to kill her?

She couldn't fight it any longer. She would stay hidden, but that was her last plan. She was out of plans...

D1381835

Have you read these special Point Horror collections yet?

Point Horror

HIDE AND SEEK

Jane McFann

■SCHOLASTIC

To my parents, who teach me life-long lessons in love,
strength and the importance of family
and to James A. Hoosty, R.K.

Scholastic Children's Books,
Commonwealth House, 1-19 New Oxford Street,
London, WC1A 1NU, UK
a division of Scholastic Publications Ltd
London ~ New York ~ Toronto ~ Sydney ~ Auckland

First published in the US by Scholastic Inc., 1995
First published in the UK by Scholastic Ltd, 1997

Text copyright © Jane McFann, 1995

ISBN: 0 590 19067 9

All rights reserved

Printed by Cox & Wyman, Reading, Berks

2 4 6 8 10 9 7 5 3 1

This book is sold subject to the condition that it shall not, by way of
trade or otherwise, be lent, resold, hired out, or otherwise circulated
without the publisher's prior consent in any form of binding or cover
other than that in which it is published and without a similar condition,
including this condition, being imposed upon the subsequent purchaser.

The End

Sixteen is too young to die, Lissa thought, but then again these were unusual circumstances. Actually, it would be a relief. She had tried everything she could think of to avoid dying. Now she was hidden in the last place she could find to hide, and she knew that it wasn't good enough.

The footsteps were getting closer.

Bird stirred in her hand, and she stroked his head soothingly. She hoped that he would not call out and give away her location — that would only speed the inevitable. Bird, however, relaxed in her hand, cooing softly. She could not unfold her hand or move her head to look at him. She didn't need to. She knew every iridescent green feather on his small body, the head blue on top shading to gray. He was about four inches tall and weighed only ounces, a gray-cheeked parrot, a breed known for its intelligent, feisty nature and its ability to bond to its owner.

Bird. Her only true friend in many ways.

If she had one dying wish, it would be to get Bird to Josh's grandmother where he would be safe and loved.

Safe.

Loved.

Had she ever felt either of those?

She searched her memory for a time. She didn't find one.

Her heart filled with sadness. It shouldn't have turned out like this. When did this day, the approaching moment, become inevitable? When had the decisions that led to this point made it impossible for any other point to be reached?

Who had made those decisions?

She didn't think that she had made them, but she could no longer be sure.

The footsteps came still nearer, then veered away. She moved her hand slowly, inch by inch, until Bird was tucked under her chin, lying against her throat where she could feel his tiny heart beat.

She wondered if after death it was still possible to miss anything. *If it was*, she thought, *she would miss Bird.*

Just Bird.

Maybe Josh. The thought raced through her mind, but she willed it away. She would not think of him. This was not the time, and there would never be another time.

Not Josh.

That was impossible.

Lissa thought about books she had read where a person's life flashed before his eyes right before he died, like a sped-up movie that showed only the most important times. It wasn't that she had many significant high points to recollect, but she wanted to die with some kind of peace. That peace would only come with understanding. This was her last chance to understand.

Okay, she thought. Back to the beginning. Let me understand.

Lissa settled into the shallow nest at the base of the tree, sheltered under the thin layer of leaves that she had managed to pull over her. She stroked Bird's head slowly, rhythmically, and willed her mind to go back.

Maybe there was another explanation.

Maybe the person out there wasn't who she thought it was.

Maybe she was wrong about everything.

She knew, however, that she wasn't.

Lissa shut her eyes, welcoming the darkness, forming in her mind a screen on which to reveal her memories.

She knew that she had to begin. There wasn't time enough to wait any longer.

The Beginning

Lissa thought back to her first vivid memory. She didn't know how old she was, maybe four or five. The sharpest part of the memory was the scent of her mother's perfume. It reminded Lissa of the pink flowers that grew along the fence that were even taller than she was.

"Hush, Lissa. You have to be quiet. Daddy's working," her mother's soft voice whispered into Lissa's ear as she held her daughter tightly against her.

"I was just playing," Lissa remembered saying. "I was just splashing in my pool." Suddenly Lissa had a sharp vision of that pool, only a few feet across, made of rigid plastic decorated with brightly colored fish.

"I know, Lissa, but you have to be quiet. You can't disturb Daddy when he's working."

"Well, what *can* I do?" Lissa remembered

the frustration she'd felt. It was hot, and the water in her pool felt wonderfully cool.

"Let's go in the house, and I'll read you a book."

"No," Lissa remembered saying.

"You may not say no," her mother said, pulling back from the child. "Look at me. Look in my eyes. *You may not say no!*"

Lissa could still feel the fear that had filled her. Her mother was mad at her. She must be a very bad girl.

"I'm sorry," Lissa whispered. "I'm sorry."

Lissa's mother hugged her fiercely. "That's my good girl. What book do you want to read today?"

Lissa had tiptoed into the house, clinging to her mother's hand. Books were quiet. Books were safe. Maybe books were better than splashing in her pool on a hot summer day.

Lissa's memory stopped there. She could not remember the book they had read or anything else about that day until dinnertime.

"What was all that noise this afternoon?" she heard her father's voice rumble as he came into the house. He didn't work in the house. He worked in the fixed-up barn that was on the other side of the yard. Lissa was not allowed to go there even though it looked like a good place to play.

"Sorry, dear," her mother said apologetically. "I hope we didn't disturb your work."

Lissa remembered wondering what her father did, what this work was. Somehow she thought that maybe he was a doctor. It always seemed quiet when she went to Doctor Dan's office, so maybe her father did the same thing. Or maybe there was a library over there. The lady in the library always told the children to hush, just like her mother did.

"You know how disruptive I find noise," her father had said.

"Yes, dear, I know. Maybe tomorrow Lissa and I will go to the park."

Lissa remembered smiling. She loved the park. She could run there rather than tiptoe. If she forgot and screamed just a little as she went down the big sliding board, silver and hot and fast, nobody told her to hush. And she could swing. Lissa loved to swing. She knew how to hold onto the chains tightly with her hands so that she could lean back, letting her long hair touch the ground, looking up to the sky, watching the trees nearby zoom in and out of her vision.

More than anything, Lissa remembered wanting to fly. She wanted to launch off into the sky like a bird and flap her wings and just fly and fly and fly. She wouldn't make any noise at all. She would just fly to those trees way over there and go to the very top and look down on the world. Nobody would see her because she would hide in the leaves.

Hide in the leaves. Lissa jolted back to the present, almost crying out at the irony. When she was a little girl and wanted to hide in the leaves, the leaves were fresh and green and touching the sky. She shifted slightly, trying to ease the ache in her spine from the hard earth and stones beneath her nest where the roots of the big tree were somewhat hollowed out. The leaves under which she was hiding were now dead, having fallen through the crisp October air. Lissa shivered, making sure that Bird was covered by her hand. He was a tropical bird, meant to live in jungles in South America where his bright green feathers would blend in with the brilliant foliage. He was supposed to live there or else in the warmth of a home. He was not meant to be out in the cold of October.

Lissa would shelter him for as long as she could. She would keep him warm.

Another part of her memory nagged at her. She remembered the thrill of leaning back so far in the swing that her hair touched the ground. That had been part of the game of swinging.

When had she ever had long hair? Somehow it seemed that she had always had shortly cropped hair, barely covering her ears and never touching her neck.

Elf hair, Josh called it.

Josh. No. She'd promised herself no Josh memories.

Lissa suddenly realized that she wanted long hair. She wanted to feel the sweep of it across her back. She wanted to feel it blow behind her in the wind. She wanted to dance naked in the moonlight with her hair flying wildly.

But there would be no time for that.

The footsteps were back.

The Beginning,
Part II

Lissa didn't want to listen to the footsteps.
They veered away, faster, angrier, crunching
more than at the start when each footstep had
been quiet, seeming to be carefully placed to
avoid warning her.

Now the footsteps were careless but confident. Lissa was near. Lissa was trapped.

Lissa would die soon.

She felt Bird begin to stir against her throat
under her hand. She cooed softly to him. Just
a little longer, she thought. Sleep a little
longer, small green bird. Then it won't matter.

She felt tears beginning to form, and she
willed herself to go back to her memories.
Even if they weren't happy, they were better
than thinking about the footsteps. They were
better than thinking about the face that she
would soon see.

Back, back she dragged her thoughts. Back

to her hair. She remembered vividly the day that her hair had been cut. It wasn't the same day as her first memory, but Lissa didn't think it was much after that. She was still little, still not in school yet. She knew that because in her first grade picture she had short hair.

Her father had been working all day, and when he came into the house, she and her mother were sitting in the kitchen. Lissa remembered the kitchen. It had white curtains at the window over the sink, and the floor was like a black and white checkerboard. Some days her mother let her play hopscotch on the kitchen floor. When her father came in that day, he had a frown on his face, and he yanked open the refrigerator, then slammed the door shut without taking anything out. Lissa remembered being startled by his sudden entrance and rapid motions. She had been sitting on one of the chairs at the kitchen table, and her mother had been braiding her long, dark hair. One half was braided, fastened and tied at the bottom with Lissa's favorite blue ribbon. Her mother was brushing the other half, beginning to divide it into threes for the braiding.

"Don't even ask how it went today," her father shouted. "I don't know why I even try. Nothing ever goes right."

"Now honey, it will be all right," her mother

said, and Lissa could feel her hair being brushed harder. "You'll find a way through the hard parts. You always do."

"That's easy for you to say," he snapped, pulling open cabinet doors and then slamming them shut.

I'd get in a lot of trouble for making that much noise, Lissa thought.

"Doesn't Lissa look beautiful?" her mother asked. "Her hair is just washed and dried, and now we're braiding it."

Her father wheeled around, facing them directly for the first time. He stared at Lissa. She could still remember his eyes. They were so dark that they looked black, and she felt like they could burn holes right through her.

I'm being quiet, Lissa thought. I'm being very quiet.

"I hate long hair," her father said, still staring at her, his voice scary quiet, worse than the shouting. "Cut it."

"Now honey, you don't mean that. Just wait until I finish braiding it. You'll see how nice it looks. We'll even pin up her braids if you'd like."

Lissa remembered clutching the other blue ribbon tightly in her hand, the ribbon meant for the bottom of her second braid.

"Don't tell me what I mean. Don't you ever

think that you know better than I do what I mean," her father said, almost whispering. "Cut it, or I will."

Lissa tried to be so quiet that she would disappear. Maybe if she didn't move, didn't even breathe, her father would forget about her.

"I'm sorry you've had a bad day," her mother said soothingly. "Lissa and I will leave for a while so that you can unwind."

Lissa knew that her mother was trying to help, but it didn't work. Her father savagely yanked open the top kitchen drawer, the one to the right of the sink where they had odds and ends of everything. He came toward them, holding the scissors with the orange handles. Lissa remembered using them very carefully to cut out pictures just a day or so before.

Lissa didn't move, even though she wanted to run. She didn't look, didn't breathe, didn't make a noise. Neither did her mother.

Her father crossed the kitchen in several big steps and grabbed her braid, the one that was finished and tied with the pretty blue ribbon. He cut it off right up close to her head, then threw the braid down on the table and put the scissors back in the drawer and walked out of the house.

Lissa looked at the braid in horror. It was

as if her father had cut off a part of her body, an arm or something. Her mother knelt beside her chair and wrapped Lissa in her arms. "I'm sorry," she said, over and over again. "I'm sorry, baby."

Lissa wasn't sure then exactly what her mother was sorry for. She wasn't the one who had cut off her braid. Lissa unclenched her fist, the one holding the other blue ribbon, and turned away from her mother's arms to lay it carefully next to her amputated braid.

Lissa remembered going to the car with her mother, driving to town and going to a lady who cut off the rest of her hair. "I'm sorry to have to cut it so short," the lady said, "but this part is cropped so close."

"It's fine," her mother said. "Lissa and I think she'll look beautiful with short hair. It will be cool and easy to take care of."

Lissa remembered the feeling of her hair falling away, seeing it on the floor where the lady was walking. It made her sad.

Afterwards her mother took her to get ice cream, but Lissa had no memory of what she had gotten. She didn't think that she had eaten it.

She only knew that she didn't feel beautiful, and that she stayed very, very quiet.

"It will be okay," her mother whispered to

her that night when she tucked her in. "It will be all right. I promise you. He's just high-strung."

Lissa remembered wondering what "high-strung" meant. She didn't ask.

Unintentionally now, her memories sprang forward and she remembered the first day that she started at her new high school this fall. She was brand new in a school where everybody already had their friendships and their routines. She didn't expect anybody to talk to her, and she didn't want to talk to anybody. All she wanted to do was go to class, learn what was expected of her, and disappear again.

"Great hair," a male voice had said as she sat in second period English class.

Lissa did nothing, hoping that the comment had not been intended for her.

"Hey, really, nice hair," the voice repeated, and this time she felt a hand lightly touch the back of her head.

She wheeled around, glaring. "Don't ever touch me," she said softly.

"Hey, sorry," the boy said. Lissa remembered how startled she had been at his hair. It was blond and hung in fuzzy locks over his ears and into his eyes. "I didn't know your name." He smiled broadly. "I'm Josh."

Lissa had turned around in her seat, saying nothing.

"Hey, sorry. I didn't mean to offend you."

Still Lissa said nothing.

Why had Josh ever talked to her again?

Why was he intruding now on her memories?

Why were the footsteps returning, coming closer, closer?

Chapter 1

Lissa held her breath, thinking that surely the footsteps would come to her this time.

They didn't, though. Once again they veered away, faster, harsher, the sound of them exploding in her ears. She was certain that they would awaken Bird, but he seemed deep in sleep, secure in the warmth of her hand, against her throat, tucked in safety.

Little did he know. Little did Bird know about how little she could do to protect him. If she couldn't save herself, how could she save him?

I'm sorry, she thought. I'm sorry that I'm not strong enough.

It was time to return to her memories. I need to go faster, she thought. I haven't much time, and I need to think through it all. If I am to understand, I need to remember.

Abby, she suddenly thought. She hadn't

thought of Abby in many years. Once she did have a friend.

Lissa had met Abby in the first grade, and they had immediately become friends. Looking back, Lissa wasn't sure why. She remembered their first conversation on the elementary school playground.

"Hi. I'm Abby. I can hit you in the face and make you cry." The words had startled Lissa, especially since the girl saying them was even smaller than Lissa, a tiny girl with long red hair and a delicate face.

"I'm Lissa."

"So want me to hit you in the face and make you cry?"

"No," Lissa had whispered.

"What did you say? Can't hear you."

"No," Lissa had repeated, only a little louder.

"Think I will anyway," Abby said, coming right up to Lissa, waving her fist in Lissa's face.

Lissa didn't move, hands at her side, eyes down.

"Hey. Hey! Aren't you going to fight back? What good are you?"

Lissa said nothing. She remained very quiet. Maybe this noisy girl would go away and leave her alone.

Not Abby. "Okay, I'll hit you in the face and make you cry another day. Let's go swing."

Now there was something that Lissa could do. She could swing. The two little girls had climbed onto swings next to each other, and immediately Lissa headed for the sky.

"Hey. Hey! You can swing good. How did you get up there so fast?"

Lissa didn't answer, leaning back. She couldn't touch her short hair to the ground, but she still leaned way, way back.

Soon Abby was just as high as Lissa, pumping her legs frantically. "Hey. Hey! Think if I jumped now I'd get to the edge of the grass over there? Do you? Do you?"

Lissa looked with alarm. The edge of the grass was far away. Lissa immediately began to slow down, not pumping to stay high, hoping that Abby would slow down, too.

"I think I could, but I'd probably break something," Abby announced. "And if I broke something, then I couldn't go to the beach next weekend. But I could get to the edge of the grass if I really wanted to."

Lissa nodded, but Abby probably didn't notice.

"And if I couldn't go to the beach, then my parents would probably leave me home with my grandmother and just take my brother to the beach, and I would hate that."

Lissa slowed down to a gentle sway.

Abby continued. "So then I'd probably have to break my brother so that he couldn't go to the beach either, and then my parents wouldn't be able to leave two broken kids with my grandmother because her nerves aren't that great these days, and then they couldn't go to the beach either and they've already paid good money for the hotel and everything. Paid good money, that's what my father always says."

Lissa stared at Abby in amazement. Didn't she ever stop talking?

"My father sells insurance. He goes to people and tells them that they need to pay money in case something bad happens like they get their hand cut off or their house burns down. What does your father do? Hey. Hey! Answer me. Didn't your mother tell you that it's polite to answer?"

Both girls stopped swinging, and Abby twisted her swing sideways on its chains so that she faced Lissa. "What does your father do?"

"I don't know," Lissa whispered.

"What do you mean you don't know what your own father does? Oh," Abby said suddenly. "Are your parents divorced or something?"

"No," Lissa said, thinking she knew what divorced meant from a show she'd seen on television. "I just don't know."

"Well, does he go to work every day wearing a tie? Does he carry his lunch in a brown bag?"

"No," Lissa said. "He goes to the barn."

"The barn? Your father is a farmer? You live on a farm? Do you have cows and chickens and pigs and stuff? That's great. Can I come visit?"

"No," Lissa said quickly. "We don't live on a farm. We just have this place we call the barn and my father goes there and stays inside all day."

"But what does he *do*?" Abby insisted. "What does he *do* inside the barn all day?"

"I don't know," Lissa said, not liking this conversation. Couldn't they talk about something else? She got off the swing and started to walk across the playground. Abby came after her, running in circles around her.

"Why don't you know? Don't you go see him? Doesn't he take you with him?"

"No," Lissa said quickly. "He needs for it to be quiet."

"But *why*?" Abby asked impatiently. "Don't you go sneak over and peek?"

"No," Lissa said, frightened at the thought. "No."

"Well, I would," Abby announced. "Let's do it. I'll come to your house and we'll peek."

"Oh no," Lissa said quickly.

"Why not? Don't you want to know? Don't you want to find out what your father does in the barn?"

Lissa thought about that. She didn't want to know. She only knew that she had to be quiet, and that she was safe with her mother when her father was working, whatever it was that he did. When he was working, he didn't yell at her and tell her that she was noisy.

"Hey. Hey! Let's find out. Okay?"

"No," Lissa repeated.

"Why not? Would he beat you? Would he make you go to bed with no supper?"

"My father doesn't beat me," Lissa said softly. He didn't. He yelled when she was bad, and he cut off her braid, but he didn't hit her. He had never hit her.

"You ask your mother and I'll ask my mother if I can come home with you tomorrow," Abby said, running away before Lissa could answer.

Lissa never asked. She had never had a friend come over to her house.

She had never had a friend.

Especially not a noisy, little red-haired girl who asked too many questions.

The next day when Lissa got on the yellow bus to go home, there was Abby. It had rained earlier and they had been kept inside for recess. They weren't in the same first grade class. Lissa had been relieved not to have seen Abby.

When Lissa got off the bus, Abby got off right after her. "My mother said fine," she said cheerfully.

Lissa stared at her in shock. What would happen? What was she going to do with this girl? This was not good. She knew that for sure.

"I don't think today is okay," Lissa said quietly.

"Well, what am I supposed to do? The bus is gone. I have to come home with you," Abby said. "Let's go."

What choice did Lissa have? She slowly walked down the lane that led to her house. Abby bounded around beside her, darting this way and that to check out flowers and rocks and birds.

"Is that it?" Abby asked as they approached the white house with the tall pink flowers. "Is that it? Why, that's a pretty house but it sure isn't a farm."

"No," Lissa said.

"But that's okay if it isn't a farm. Where's the barn where your father works?"

"We can't go there."

"I know, but where is it?"

Lissa didn't answer. She pulled open the door and walked into the kitchen, wishing that Abby would be more quiet.

"Lissa, is that you?" her mother called.

"Yes," Lissa answered, worried.

"Me, too," Abby hollered.

Lissa flinched.

Her mother's footsteps rapidly approached.

"Hi," Abby said, smiling. "I'm Abby. My mother said that it was fine if I visited Lissa today. If you need for her to pick me up, this is her number." Abby pulled a piece of paper out of her pocket and gave it to Lissa's mother. "If you want to take me home, that's fine, too. She wrote down our address. This is a very nice house. Do you think I might have a drink? Water would be fine. I don't mean to make any extra work."

Her mother stared in amazement at Abby, who walked rapidly from one side of the kitchen to the other, looking at everything.

"Lissa, why didn't you tell me that you were bringing a friend home with you?" her mother asked her.

"I didn't know," she whispered.

"I sort of invited myself," Abby said cheerfully. How had she heard Lissa? "My mother says that I'm very forward. She says that I'll go far in life, though. She says that the world better watch out for Abby Marshall."

Lissa's mother looked at her in amazement.

"Do you think Lissa and I could go out in the yard? It sure does look nice out there. My yard's all filled up with a swing set and sand box and stuff like that because my brother's only four. Your yard looks very nice."

"Lissa's father is working, and he needs for it to be quiet," her mother said hesitantly. "Maybe you girls could go up to Lissa's room."

"Oh, we'll be very quiet," Abby said in an exaggerated whisper. "Nobody will ever know that we're out there."

"Well, I suppose for a few minutes," her mother said. She walked out into the yard, and Lissa followed Abby as she practically tiptoed around the yard, asking in whispers about the flowers and the trees. Lissa's mother answered her quietly. Lissa could see Abby's eyes turn again and again to the small red barn at the far side of the yard.

Finally Abby sat down under the big elm tree, motioning for her to sit down, too. "If you have things you need to do, we'll be fine," she said to Lissa's mother. "We'll just sit here real quiet and look at the sky."

"Well, I do need to start dinner."

"Don't let us stop you," Abby said.

"I'll come check on you in a few minutes," Lissa's mother said, looking over at the barn and then back at the girls. Lissa knew how important it was for her mother to have dinner ready when her father came in. He didn't like to wait.

The minute Lissa's mother was back in the house, Abby got up. "Come on," she said, grabbing the reluctant girl's hand. "Let's go."

"Where?" Lissa asked, with a sick feeling that she knew where Abby meant.

"The barn," she said, forgetting to whisper, then clapping her hand over her mouth. "The barn," she whispered. "Come on before your mother comes back."

"No," Lissa said.

"Then I'll go by myself," Abby announced.

Somehow that seemed even worse. Reluctantly Lissa followed her as she walked across the yard. The kitchen window didn't look out on this side. She almost wished it did so that her mother would stop Abby.

When they got closer to the barn, Abby started to tiptoe. Lissa's heart was thumping as she followed. She expected her father to come roaring out, yelling at them. Abby circled until they were on the side of the barn away from the house. Part way down the wall there was a dirty, small window, but it was too high for Abby to see into. Lissa sighed with relief. Now they could go back to the tree.

"Lissa, lift me up," Abby whispered.

How could she talk? How could she make noise this close to the barn? Lissa frantically shook her head no.

"Lissa, don't you want to know? Lift me up. I just need to be a little bit higher. I know. Kneel down and I'll climb up on your back."

She was making too much noise. Lissa's father was going to hear. Lissa started to feel sick. Abby shoved down on her shoulder impatiently. Lissa knelt on her hands and knees. She felt Abby climb up, felt Abby's feet on her back, felt Abby lift up on her tiptoes.

Then Lissa heard her gasp.

She jumped down off Lissa's back and started to run.

Chapter 2

What had Abby seen in the barn? What had made her gasp? What had made her run? Frightened as Lissa was that her father would hear them, she wanted to know. She wanted to look in the window.

She followed after Abby as she dashed back to the tree and flung herself down on the ground under it. "What did you see?" Lissa asked her. "What did you see?"

"Sshh," Abby said. Something must have scared her. It wasn't like Abby to tell anybody to be quiet.

"Was it terrible?" Lissa asked. Maybe her father really was a doctor and there were bodies and blood and stuff in the barn.

"I can't explain," Abby said. "I don't know how to explain."

"Then I have to see, too," Lissa said. She didn't know where the courage came from.

She didn't know what made her willing to go back across that yard and risk being found by her father. She had never wanted to know before. But that was before Abby. Now Abby knew and she didn't. That didn't seem fair or right.

"Your mother will probably be out soon," Abby said, looking toward the house.

She knew Abby was right, but she needed to know. "Come on," she said, beginning to walk back across the yard. Reluctantly, lagging behind, Abby followed. Once they were back at the window, Abby slowly got to her knees and braced her arms. Lissa crawled up on Abby's skinny back, then put her hands against the barn for support and carefully got up to her feet. Lissa couldn't breathe, and she had to will herself to move.

She looked through the window and saw her father. She almost lost her balance because he was closer than she had imagined, but it was his back that was toward the window. She looked beyond him.

Then she saw what had made Abby gasp. Her father was painting a huge picture, the biggest picture that she had ever seen. To her it looked like it was as big as the wall in her bedroom, and her father was splashing on paint with a brush.

It was the picture itself that scared her. It was all big slashes of red and orange and green, but mostly red. It didn't look like the pictures in books or at school. It didn't have flowers or trees or houses or people. It just had paint splashed all over in jagged lines, almost like lightning had hit her father's picture.

Most of all, it looked angry. It reminded her of her father the day he had cut off her hair. It reminded her of how his voice sounded when he yelled.

Lissa got off of Abby's back, and she, too, ran. Abby followed her, and neither of them stopped until they were back at the tree, throwing themselves on their backs, faces to the sky, panting.

"Did you see?" Abby finally asked when their breathing was normal again.

"Yes," Lissa answered.

"What do you think it's supposed to be?" Abby asked.

"I don't know," she answered, not wanting to talk about her hair or the yelling.

"I guess this means that your father is an artist," Abby said, saying the word as if it were special, almost like president or something.

"I guess so," Lissa said softly. Her father was an artist. She rolled the thought around in her head, getting used to it. Her father was an artist. He painted pictures. Big pictures. Big red pictures.

"That's neat," Abby said, but there was hesitation in her voice.

"Artists need for it to be quiet," Lissa said, fitting that piece together.

"Oh," Abby said. Then she was silent for a minute. "It's a good thing my father isn't an artist," she finally burst out. "My little brother hollers all the time, and we always have other kids in our yard, and we make noise every day. If my father was an artist, he'd never get one tiny little picture done, sure not a big huge one like your father is doing. Good thing my father sells insurance."

With that Lissa's mother came out the door and crossed the yard toward them. "I don't think we should tell her we peeked," Lissa whispered quickly.

"Okay," Abby agreed.

Her mother took them back into the kitchen with her, and they baked chocolate chip cookies. Lissa remembered the smell of them, and she remembered Abby eating about twenty. Her mother fixed Abby a bag of them to take home. Lissa remembered that they took Abby home before dinner. Part of her had wanted

Abby to stay and eat with them, but part of her wanted Abby to go away before her father came in. Her father the artist.

Lissa remembered that day vividly. Maybe she remembered it so well because Abby never came back to her house. She was not sure why. Lissa thought that Abby had found another friend. She seemed to remember that Abby became best friends with a girl who could run as fast as she could, and that the two of them always got in trouble on the playground during recess.

Maybe she was scared away by Lissa's father's painting.

Maybe she knew that she couldn't stay quiet enough to be at Lissa's house.

Anyway, Abby never came back. In fact, it was years before another person ever came to visit Lissa at her house.

And that was another day that she would never forget.

Chapter 3

Footsteps. Where were the footsteps? She listened and heard nothing. Maybe they were gone. Maybe this nightmare was over. Maybe she was safe.

Or maybe this was a trick. Maybe the whole idea was for her to believe that she was safe and come out.

Besides, she wasn't safe. She was never going to be safe. Who was she trying to kid?

Where was she going to run? Where else was left to hide? She had run out of answers to those questions a little while ago, back when she found the big tree with the hollow at its roots, when she curled into the rough little nest and pulled the leaves over her.

Bird stirred in her hand, almost as if he were dreaming. How much longer would he stay quiet? Somehow that didn't worry her. Even if Bird didn't give her away, she would still be found.

She didn't want to think about it anymore. She didn't want to look forward to what awaited her. She'd rather go back again, back to her memories.

Where had she left off? Abby, she remembered. What was next in her chain of memories? What was the next link? She searched for the next piece of the puzzle that was her life.

She remembered that for a long time she kept it a secret that she knew her father was an artist. Somehow she convinced herself that it was normal not to know about where her father went and what he did. She never went back to peek in the barn again. She didn't want to see that painting again.

It must have been a long time later, maybe years, before she and her mother talked about what her father did. She remembered that because it was one of the good times, one of the happy times. She remembered that she and her mother were in the kitchen waiting for her father to come in for dinner when the phone rang. From her mother's side of the conversation, Lissa knew that it must be good news because she kept saying, "That's wonderful. I'm sure he'll be happy to hear that."

Her father came in a few minutes later, and

her mother threw herself into his arms. She whispered something in his ear, and then Lissa's father picked her mother up in his arms and danced with her around the kitchen. Lissa watched in amazement. She had never seen her parents behave this way before. Her father was laughing. Lissa was not sure that she had ever heard her father laugh before. She remembered thinking how little her mother looked in comparison to her father. Her mother was hugging him and telling him she always knew it would happen.

What would happen? Lissa wanted to know, but she stayed quiet. They had forgotten she was there. Finally she went to her bedroom. It was a long time before her mother came to look for her, and her face was still smiling.

"Sorry, Lissa, but your father and I had to celebrate and I forgot about dinner. Come down. We'll eat in a few minutes."

Lissa went down the stairs, and the kitchen was empty. "Where is he?" she asked.

"Oh, he went back to the barn. He'll probably be working all night now."

"Why?" she asked, getting up her courage. "What is he doing?"

"You really don't know, do you?" her mother said, suddenly looking at her. "You don't understand all of this, do you?"

"No," she said, waiting.

"Your father paints wonderful pictures," her mother said, whirling around the kitchen, practically skipping. "He's been waiting and waiting to get the critical recognition that he deserves."

Lissa remembered not being sure what she meant, but she let her go on without interruption.

"Well, today one of the best small galleries of contemporary art in New York just decided to feature his work in a show. This is it, Lissa. This is the break that he needs."

"So he has to go back to the barn?" Lissa asked.

"He has two paintings that he needs to finish in time to ship them to New York next week, so he'll practically have to work around the clock. But it's worth it, Lissa. This will make all the difference in the world."

"Will it make him happy?" Lissa asked. Maybe he would laugh again. Maybe he'd even spend time with her.

Her mother gave her a funny look, part happy and part sad all mixed together. "Yes, Lissa, I hope it will make him happy."

"Is it hard to be an artist?" Lissa asked. Maybe that was why he always seemed so angry with her.

"Yes, I think it is," her mother said. "Some days nothing goes right, and sometimes he doesn't think that other people will ever like his work."

Lissa remembered the painting with the slashes of red and orange and green. Would other people like that? Or would it scare them the way it scared her?

Suddenly she looked around the kitchen and thought about the rest of the house. There was nothing on their walls that was anything like the painting she had seen in the barn. "Why don't we have his paintings in our house?" she asked.

"He says he can't stand to live with his mistakes," her mother said, shaking her head. "He wants everything to be perfect, and if it isn't, he hates it."

The idea came to her in a flash. Maybe she wasn't perfect, and that was why he hated her.

Did he hate her? Did her father hate her? She had never thought of that before. She knew that he often seemed mad at her, but she figured it was her fault because she wasn't quiet enough or good enough.

But now she had to be perfect or he would hate her. What did that mean? How could she be perfect? What would make her father love her?

"Smile, Lissa," her mother said, giving her a big hug. "This means that we'll get to go to New York for a big opening, and everybody will say wonderful things about your father's work, and we'll get lots of money."

"And live happily ever after like in the books?" she whispered.

"And live happily ever after," her mother said fiercely. "Trust me, Lissa. Everything will be fine now."

But it wasn't fine.

She remembered a while later, maybe days or weeks, hearing her parents fighting in their bedroom one night.

"I'm not taking a child with us to New York," her father's voice boomed.

"Let her share in this," her mother answered. "Besides, where would we leave her? It's not like we have family or friends here."

"I don't care what you do with her, but I don't want to worry about a child."

"You won't have to worry about her," her mother said soothingly. "I'll take care of her. Besides, she behaves wonderfully. You'll hardly know she's there."

Lissa cried herself to sleep that night. She remembered wondering if her parents would just leave her home by herself. She sort of wanted them to. She could fix her own meals and take care of the house. She wouldn't have to worry about being perfect.

They did, though, end up taking her to New York with them, and she remembered her father yelling in the car nearly the whole way there.

"He's just nervous," her mother whispered to her after one particularly bad scene. "He's just excited about the show."

Lissa nodded, saying nothing.

Lissa remembered that they had two big hotel rooms right next to each other. She had never stayed in a hotel before, and she was both frightened and excited by the view. The window looked down on busy city streets from twenty stories high, and there was a constant flow of taxis and cars and bicycles and people. She'd never seen anything like it. Her mother helped her to unpack and get settled, running back and forth from Lissa's room to the one next door.

That night they all went to the opening. Her mother made sure that Lissa was ready in her new navy-blue dress, and then she went next door. Lissa nearly gasped when she and her father came back a few minutes later. Her mother looked beautiful in a black dress that sparkled at the neck and the wrists. Her hair was twisted up, and she looked like a movie star. Her father looked like she had never seen him before. He was wearing a soft black sweater and black pants that were loose and beautiful, and he had on a jacket with gray and black and blue in it. His thick gray hair was brushed straight back. She wasn't sure what an artist was supposed to look like, but somehow he looked like one.

They took a taxi to the gallery, and Lissa remembered being frightened by the taxi driver's cursing and swerving. Her mother just laughed and held her hand. The art gallery had many rooms with high white walls and lights in the ceiling. Everywhere there were her father's paintings. Lissa saw the one that he had been painting the day that she and Abby had peeked. It nearly filled one big wall, and lots of people were in front of it, looking up. All the walls were covered with paintings that were filled with slashes of color: black and green and orange and purple and most of all red. There was red everywhere.

There were lots of people with glasses in their hands and wearing brightly colored, swirly clothes or else dressed all in black. They chatted and laughed and used words Lissa didn't really understand: neo-impressionism, visceral, post-imagistic. After a while, the words swirled around her just like the colors did. Her mother tried to keep hold of her, but after a while she found a corner that had a counter and a desk. She sat in a little chair there and watched. Her mother checked on Lissa every now and then, but mainly she dashed off to talk to people or to stand proudly next to Lissa's father.

Her father smiled. He shook hands and drank from his glass and smiled. From the look on his face, people were saying nice things about his paintings.

Lissa wondered if people would buy them and take them home and hang them in their houses. She wondered if they would want to live with all that red.

That night her mother tucked her into bed and then went next door. "Your father won't be able to sleep. He needs me to keep him company," she said when Lissa asked her mother to stay with her.

As soon as the door shut behind her mother, Lissa went to the window and looked down. She watched all the people that were still on the streets, even though it was very late. There were still lights and life and commotion. When did these people sleep?

She watched for hours, finally falling asleep herself with her head on the windowsill of the hotel room in New York City.

Chapter 4

Bird awoke with a start. Lissa listened carefully to see what he had heard. She didn't hear the footsteps. She didn't hear anything other than the normal sounds of the woods: birds at a distance, the scurrying of squirrels.

Bird pried his way out of her hand, grabbing at the leaves with his beak. She could understand his confusion. What were they doing there on the ground, covered with leaves? Bird made his way over to her shoulder, ducking under the leaves that he didn't toss out of his way. Lissa could feel his sharp toenails snag in her sweater as he climbed down her shoulder and on to the ground.

Don't leave me, Bird, she said silently. Don't you leave me, too. Don't leave me to die alone.

She would have wanted him to go if she thought that there was a chance that he could survive. What chance did he have, though? He was a small green tropical bird with clipped wings. He was no more than a mouthful for the first cat or fox or hawk that spotted him. Besides, if he didn't get killed, he would die from the chill.

Poor Bird. As soon as he got to the ground, he must have felt the cold of the earth because he came clambering back up. He came back up to where Lissa's hand was still curled against her throat and nudged under her fingers. Still, he wasn't happy. He made his complaining noise, almost a low growling. Normally she heard it when she was late feeding him in the morning.

He was probably hungry. As if from a distance, as if noticing it for a body other than her own, Lissa realized that she, too, was hungry. What difference did it make? She was going to die, and it didn't really matter if she died hungry or full.

It did matter, though, if she died with some clue as to why she was dying. She didn't want her death to be some random act of destruction, meaningless, impersonal.

There was a reason for this, and it was up to her to find it. It was time to go back again.

What was next after the gallery opening in New York? What was next? Their lives had changed after that, at least in some ways. Her mother told her that the reviews of her father's show had been excellent, and that buyers were lining up for his work. All that it meant for Lissa was that her father spent more and more time in the barn, and that they had more money. She and her mother went shopping more often, and she bought Lissa hard-backed books with beautiful pictures.

Otherwise, nothing was very different. Her father still came in from the barn in a terrible mood most days, and she still spent a lot of time in her room. That was okay, though, because her mother had bought her a beautiful four-poster bed with a white canopy over it. Lissa thought it was the most wonderful bed in the world, and she would lie there for hours at a time, dreaming of lands where people could fly and live in the trees and clouds.

Josh. No. Not Josh memories. Josh was not a part of that life. She didn't meet Josh until this year, only months ago. She was not to that time yet, not nearly there. Not Josh.

Still, he was all she could remember right now. She thought he would never speak to her again, he of the weird blond locks of hair and the goofy grin. After all, she had told him to leave her alone, and she never turned around to speak to him in English class. Besides, why would he see her? Nobody else did. She had worked on being invisible until she had it down to nearly an art. Every day she wore jeans and sweaters, nothing that would stand out, and she never participated in class. She did all her work and got good grades, which satisfied the teachers, and she kept totally to herself, which kept everyone else at a distance.

That was the way she wanted it. That was the way it had to be. She knew then that there was danger, and that attention was the most dangerous thing of all.

Still, there was Josh. She'd never know why. She'd never have a chance to ask. She was sitting in English class, half listening to the teacher, half daydreaming. English was easy for her. After spending most of her life reading books, she read quickly and well, and she loved to write. She sat in her seat, not intruding on the discussion that swirled around her, and she drew. With a very sharp pencil on a small piece of paper, she created the world that she imagined when she dreamed in her canopy bed. She drew tiny little trees with birds hidden in them, and miniature houses out of which peeked rabbits and squirrels. Flowers bloomed in every crack and crevice, and tucked into the very littlest of spaces were fairies and elves. The challenge she gave herself was to make them almost invisible. They had to blend into their worlds so completely that at first or second or third glance, they didn't even exist. It was only the careful observer, the one who knew how to see, that would find them.

Lissa had been drawing for years, scene after scene after scene. Nobody yet had found the fairies.

Then again, nobody had seen her drawings except for one person.

It had been a mistake. She had been drawing in her bedroom, whiling away a summer's afternoon, and her mother had called to her. She stuck her drawing in a book and ran down the steps, book in hand, to see what her mother had wanted. It turned out that she wanted Lissa to help weed the flowerbeds, and Lissa had left the book on the kitchen table. She loved to help with the flowers, her mother patiently showing her which were weeds and which were flowers, telling her the names, showing her how to tell one from another. Lissa always studied the flowers carefully, trying to learn how the petals were put together so that she could draw them later in her secret pictures.

Sometimes she thought that she would show her pictures to her mother, but she always stopped. Her mother thought Lissa's father's paintings were wonderful, and they were the opposite of what Lissa drew, huge and bright, where her pictures were tiny and drawn only in pencil. Besides, they weren't perfect. They shouldn't be seen if they weren't perfect. Sometimes the fairies could be found too easily, or the flowers didn't turn out quite right, or the rabbits had eyes that were too big or necks that were too long. She never allowed herself to erase. If it wasn't right, she tore it up and started again.

She and her mother were still in the yard, deep into one of the flowerbeds, when her father came storming out of the barn.

"I'm sorry, honey, did we bother you?" her mother said. After all, she had been talking to Lissa, and maybe her voice had carried.

"I'll never meet the deadline for that commission," her father shouted, slamming into the house. "I need something to eat."

Lissa and her mother quickly got up and headed inside. Lissa remembered looking back longingly at the flowers.

Her father was sitting at the kitchen table, head in his hands, when they got there. Her mother immediately began to move from refrigerator to counter, taking out the ingredients for a summer salad. Lissa didn't know whether to help her or to go to her room. Her mother solved her confusion by asking her to set the table. She handed Lissa the plates, and she carefully put them on the table, avoiding her father by putting his plate in the center of the table. With a sigh, he raised his head and flung out his arm, knocking Lissa's book off the table. She immediately bent down to get it, but he beat her to it. Lissa's drawing had shaken loose from the book.

She remembered thinking it looked naked there on the black and white checkerboard of the kitchen floor. She desperately wanted to rescue it, to hide it.

Her father picked it up. He studied her careful, tiny drawing, then snorted. "What's this trite garbage?" he asked. "Somebody's been reading too much of that fantasy crap." He crumpled up the paper and threw it across the kitchen.

Lissa never said a word. She crossed the kitchen, picked up the wad of paper that was her drawing, and threw it in the trash can under the sink. Then she finished setting the table.

For a long time after that, she didn't draw any more. Then she started again, just as a way to relieve the boredom while she sat in school. She never kept the pictures that she drew. They were just a way to waste time. As soon as she had filled the paper with the tiny little world, she crumpled it up and threw it away.

That is, until Josh. Lissa was sitting in English, almost finished with a drawing, when a hand lunged over her shoulder.

"What's that?" Josh hissed, his voice covered by the heated discussion going on in class. "What are you drawing?"

"Nothing," Lissa said, frantically covering the paper with her arm.

"No, let me see," Josh insisted. "It looked cool. Please, Lissa. Let me see."

"No," she said, afraid that the teacher would notice the fuss.

"I just want to see it for a minute," Josh said, puppy-like in his persistence, and he lunged over her shoulder and grabbed the corner of the paper.

Before she could grab it, he had her drawing. Her stomach ached with anger. He had no right.

There was silence behind her. Maybe he'd lose interest as soon as he saw how stupid it was. Then she could crumple it up and throw it away.

"Lissa, this is definitely wonderful," Josh said, leaning forward until his mouth was at her ear. She flinched away from him. "I've found six fairies so far. Are there more hidden in here?"

He'd found them? How had he found them? She thought she'd hidden them more carefully than that.

"How do you do this? They're so tiny. Every time I look at this, I see more cool things. Can I keep it? Do you have more of these? You should sell these or something. Where'd you learn to draw like this?"

The teacher rescued her. "Josh," she said sharply. "Am I interrupting you by teaching class?"

"No, ma'am," Josh said. "It's just . . ."

For a moment Lissa thought her heart was going to stop beating. Was he going to show the teacher her picture? Was he going to show the whole class? No. She willed her thoughts to Josh. No. No. No.

"It's just that I was kind of talking to myself," Josh said. The class laughed, familiar with Josh's off-balance way of looking at things. It never failed that while the rest of the class was talking about the main characters in a book they were reading, Josh would be all hung up on some minor character who only appeared once on page 73. Josh would want to know why he was there, and what he was doing while the rest of the book was going on, and the teacher would finally have to yank him back to the big stuff.

Still, whenever Josh started to ask a question, the whole class would get quiet and sort of expectant, waiting to see what he would come up with this time.

"When I get it all figured out, I'll share it with the rest of you," Josh said with a laugh.

"I'm sure you will," the teacher said, smiling.

Lissa sat frozen for the remaining minutes of class. When the bell rang, Josh put his hand on her shoulder. "I'm sorry I took your picture," he said as she turned around. "It's just that it was so cool that I had to have a better look at it. You're really talented, Lissa."

In response Lissa took her picture from her desk, crumpled it up, and threw it in the trash can as she walked out of the classroom.

"Lissa! Wait!" She heard Josh's voice behind her.

By the time he got to the door, though, she had melted into the crowd in the hallway and was gone.

Chapter 5

Josh kept after her. Lissa didn't know why. He was the only one. Everybody else would give up in the face of her silence, but not Josh.

When Lissa came to English class the next day, she sat down as quickly as she could and immediately buried her nose in a book. She couldn't take the chance of drawing again. The next thing she knew, other kids in the room were giggling. She didn't look up. She was positive that their good humor had nothing to do with her.

Then Josh was there. Even Lissa couldn't ignore him because he was kneeling beside her chair, looking up at her with imploring eyes and a huge grin, hair dangling in his eyes, over-sized shirt swamping his body.

What made it even worse was that he was holding a huge bouquet of flowers. Now these weren't the kind of flowers that a person buys from the florist. No, these flowers filled his arms. Some looked more like branches off of bushes; others were huge weeds from some field. Still, they were a burst of color, and they were being held out to Lissa.

"Will you forgive me, Lissa?" Josh asked, his voice dramatic and loud enough for everybody in the room to hear.

She wanted to shrink under her desk. She wanted to evaporate. She wanted to die. All she ever asked was to be ignored, and now she was the center of a huge scene with every eye in the room focused on her. She could feel her face flush red, her stomach flip.

"Lissa, I'm not getting up until you say that you forgive me," Josh said.

"What'd you do to her?" a voice called out.

"Must have been pretty bad," another voice added.

"If she doesn't want them, I'll take the flowers, Josh," a girl said flirtatiously.

"You call those flowers?" another voice laughed.

"Lissa, I wish you'd accept his apology so that I can start class." There was a note of humor in her English teacher's voice.

All Lissa wanted to do was end the scene. "I forgive you," she said softly to Josh.

"She forgives me!" Josh yelled, bouncing to

his feet and leaping into the air. Flowers went everywhere, and he then scurried to pick them up, piling them on Lissa's desk. She buried her face in them, too embarrassed to breathe.

Class began, and her heart eventually slowed its racing. "I really am sorry about yesterday." Josh had leaned forward and was whispering to her.

"It's okay," she said, hoping that would end it.

"No, it's not," he said. "I violated your privacy. Just because I have no sense of privacy doesn't mean I shouldn't respect yours."

What did he think he was doing to her privacy by staging huge scenes in front of an entire English class?

"Here. I have a present for you." He was handing her something over her shoulder, but she didn't take it.

"Aren't the flowers enough?" she hissed.

"Oh, they were just a joke," he said. "Here. Take it."

Reluctantly she reached over her shoulder. He pushed an envelope into her hand.

"Open it," he whispered.

"Not now," she said, afraid that the teacher would yell at them and she'd be embarrassed yet again.

"Now," he insisted, "or I won't believe that you forgive me."

Slowly, trying to make no noise, she unsealed the envelope and pulled out the card that was inside. A shower of tiny little silver metallic stars cascaded out. She could hear a muffled laugh from behind her. Now the small mountain of branches and flowers on her desk was glistening with little points of light. Lissa picked some of them up, clutching them in her hand.

"Open the card," insisted the voice behind her.

The card had a picture of a castle on the front. Spires and towers rose from the rock walls, and clouds surrounded the bottom of it, making it appear to float. Inside there was a quote from Henry David Thoreau: *If you have built castles in the air, your work need not be lost; that is where they should be. Now put foundations under them.*

Lissa had read that quote before, and she loved it. How had Josh known?

Then, underneath, printed in precise little letters, Josh had written:

Princess Lissa:
I am sorry I entered into your realm un-

invited. Perhaps someday you will lower the drawbridge, call off the dragons, and come down from your tower.

Josh

She turned around to look at Josh, tears in her eyes.

Chapter 6

"I'm sorry, I'm sorry, I'm sorry," he whispered. "I was trying to make you feel better, and now I've made you cry."

"It's okay," Lissa said, turning her head away. She didn't want to talk to him. She didn't want to tell him that his kindness was more than she could bear.

Luckily, the teacher gave them a quiz, and she had the rest of the period to regain her composure.

This could not be. Josh could not know. Nobody could know. That was part of the price. It had never been hard before. It was so easy to shut people out, to remove herself from them, that she had never even been tempted to talk to anyone, to tell anybody.

Who was this Josh? Why was he doing these things? Why didn't he just deal with all of those happy, normal girls who flocked around him, attracted by his silly charm? Why was he trying to get inside her life?

He couldn't. She couldn't allow that.

When the bell rang to end class, she gathered up the flowers as quickly as she could, but they were unwieldy. Besides, she was trying to pick up the little silver stars that had fallen through onto her desk.

Josh helped her. "What can I do?" he asked. "I'm having a hard time doing the right thing here."

She tried to say the words that she knew she had to say. They needed to come out of her mouth, firm and convincing: Just leave me alone. I don't want anything to do with you. Please. Don't come near me.

She tried to force the words past the lump in her throat, but they got stuck. All Josh heard was her silence.

"So I have to figure it out on my own," he said with a laugh. "That's okay. I enjoy a challenge. Enjoy the flowers." With that he dumped the rest of them into her arms and left.

Lissa got out of the room as quickly as she could, certain that the teacher's curious eyes were on her. This was not good. She was meant to be invisible. Before it had been a choice. Now it was a necessity.

She tried to remember when she had first desired to be invisible. She guessed it was after she gave up hoping that she'd be able to fly. If she couldn't escape by going away, she'd escape by going inside.

Once she remembered knocking over her glass of milk at the dinner table. It was an accident, a rare one. Usually she was very careful not to make any sudden moves, not to make noise that would draw her father's attention. This night, though, her elbow bumped the glass just hard enough to make it fall on the floor and shatter.

"How am I supposed to relax with this kind of behavior going on?" her father yelled. "I've been working all day. You'd think I could get a little peace in my own house."

"I'm sorry," Lissa whispered. She must have been maybe ten years old at the time. "I'll clean it up."

"Just get out," her father snapped. "Just leave me to finish my dinner in peace."

"But honey, Lissa hasn't finished her dinner. We'll clean up the floor in a minute," her mother said, tension in her voice.

"I'm not hungry," Lissa said, getting up from the table. "I'll go to my room."

She lay on her canopy bed, staring up at the white fabric. Why was she so clumsy? Why was she so horrible that her father couldn't even stand to eat dinner with her?

Why did her father hate her?

It had to be her fault. He wouldn't just hate her for no reason. It must be that she was ugly and clumsy and stupid and imperfect. He was an artist. He was important. He must be ashamed to have a daughter like her.

Her mother came to her room a few hours later, telling her that her father had gone back out to the barn to paint, asking her if she wanted something to eat. Lissa told her she didn't want anything.

She didn't deserve to eat.

She wondered if her mother was sorry that she was her daughter, too. Her father never seemed to yell at her mother the way he yelled at Lissa. Maybe if she weren't there, they would always be happy, like they had been in New York when he had the show in the gallery. He and her mother were together in their room without her. He had seemed happy then.

Lissa tried to figure out where she could go. She didn't have any friends. Since Abby, nobody had made the effort to talk to her or come to her house. She didn't have any family. They never visited grandparents or aunts or uncles, so she figured she didn't have any. Where could she go?

Since she couldn't figure out any answers to that, she would have to try harder to be good. She would have to be perfect. Then her father would love her. He would have to.

She figured that at least she could be perfect at school, nothing less than A's in everything. She remembered walking into the house the day that sixth grade ended, clutching her final report card. Every marking period, every subject, every single grade on that report card was an A. She was smiling to herself. There. That was perfect. Her father would have to say something good about her report card.

Her mother looked at it and told Lissa how proud she was of her. She said that she knew how much hard work went into those grades, and she said that they'd have to figure out a special treat to celebrate. Lissa thanked her, but what she really wanted was for her father to see all those perfect A's. This time it would be different. This time he would be proud of her.

When Lissa set the table for dinner that night, she left her report card right in the middle of the table. He would have to see it. In Lissa's mind, it almost glowed.

Her heart raced when he came in the kitchen door, throwing himself down in his accustomed chair at the table. He didn't look at her report card. That was okay, though. Any minute he would notice it.

She began to carry the food to the table as her mother dished it up: hamburgers, green beans, salad, rolls. She carefully placed each one so that it didn't cover her report card. He would have to notice.

He began to fill his plate with food. Lissa could hardly breathe as the anticipation built. Any moment now, any moment.

Finally her mother was the one to notice her report card. She picked it up and held it out to her father. "Look at Lissa's grades," she said proudly. "Isn't this a wonderful report card?"

Her father quickly scanned the sheet. "Sixth grade," he said. "What can be hard about sixth grade? Anybody can do well down at that level. Pass me the pepper, please."

Lissa didn't finish her dinner that night, either. She sat for a few agonizing minutes while her parents talked about some artist whose work her father hated, then excused herself from the table.

At least for once her father noticed that she was leaving. "What's wrong?" he asked. "Don't you like your mother's cooking?"

"I'm not hungry," she answered, climbing the steps to her room.

Still, year after year, she kept getting those A's. It never made any difference to her father. She guessed she never got to a level where everybody couldn't do well. She never made him proud of her.

She remembered one day when they got their report cards, some boy in her class grabbed her report card and studied it in amazement. "Man, look at all these A's," he announced. "If I took home grades like these, my parents would have heart attacks and die. But if they lived through the shock, man, they'd buy me anything I wanted. They'd frame this report card and nail it to the refrigerator. Man, what I wouldn't give for a report card like this."

Lissa wanted to give it to him. She wanted to erase her name, and put his on it instead. What difference would it make?

Still, Lissa knew that she was lucky. She knew that there was one girl, Sarah, who came to school with bruises on her arms and legs, and once in a while on her face. She always said that she fell or was wrestling with her brother or something, but there were whispers that her father beat her.

Lissa's father never touched her. He never spanked her or hit her. He never hugged her, either, but he never beat her like Sarah's father did.

She was one of the lucky ones. She had two parents, a nice house, plenty of food and clothes, lots of books to read.

Lissa was one of the lucky ones.

Wasn't she?

Chapter 7

Lissa listened carefully. Silence. Too much silence. There were not the usual noises of the woods: birds, squirrels, insects. It was completely silent. He must still be there, close by.

Deep within her, she tried to find one last burst of optimism, of courage. Maybe she still had a chance. Maybe she could tuck Bird into her hand and make a run for it. The woods were deep and confusing, but she knew some of the paths. Maybe she could find her way out, get to a house or a road, beg for help from some kind stranger.

Right. Who was she trying to fool? She didn't have a chance. Besides, even if she lived through today, there was always tomorrow.

If she didn't die today, she'd die tomorrow or the next day. There was no way to hide completely. And was that living? Was it enough to live for another day, always knowing that she was being hunted, being followed, being watched for the perfect moment to kill her?

She couldn't fight it any longer. She would stay hidden, but that was her last plan. She was out of plans.

It wasn't that she had immediately given up. No, she had tried everything she could think of to be able to survive. It just hadn't worked. She wasn't clever or strong or brave enough to find a way out of this.

Besides, she couldn't even understand. How could she find a way out of something she couldn't even understand?

She moved one finger to stroke Bird's tiny head. She envied him. He, too, would die soon, but at least he didn't know it. He could sleep peacefully, unaware that minutes from now, he would die.

Lissa knew.

What else did she know? She searched, her mind racing through images: Abby, her mother, Josh, her father. Were those the only people she knew? That was almost the truth, given how completely she had withdrawn from people.

Wait. There had been a second time when someone had come to her house to visit, uninvited, almost as Abby had. What was her name? Lissa searched her memory. The name had suited her, she had thought. Nicollette. That was it. A tall, thin, sophisticated name.

It had been right after that newspaper article that her parents had argued about one night at dinner.

"Honey, the features editor of the newspaper called today. They want to do an article on you. Isn't that exciting?" Her mother had waited until they were finishing dessert before she brought up the topic. "I told her that you would get back in touch."

"And what made you think I'd want to do that?" her father snapped.

"I thought the publicity would be good. You know, local artist builds national reputation. It might encourage some of the local art patrons to buy your work."

"You don't think I'm good enough to let my work speak for itself?" her father said, his voice harsh and critical.

"Of course I do," her mother said. "I think your work is brilliant. You know that. Still, I'd like for everybody to know what a major talent they've got right in their own backyard."

"I hate reporters," her father griped, but his voice was calmer. Her mother's flattery seemed to be working.

"I'm sure they'd send their best writer," she said. "Why don't you call them tomorrow and see what you think?"

"You do it," her father said. "I have more important things to do."

"I'll set it all up," her mother said. "I'll try to find a time that will be the least disruptive."

"Probably cost me a day's work, what with my concentration broken," her father said, but he actually smiled at her mother.

"I know how hard you work," her mother said. "People need to realize how difficult it is to be an artist."

Lissa's father's grumbling ended under her mother's patient words.

I wonder if people realize how difficult it is to be an artist's daughter, Lissa thought, keeping her head down as she ate so that she wouldn't attract her father's attention. Of course, if she were a better daughter, perhaps it wouldn't be so difficult. He seemed to be able to get along with her mother.

Of course, her mother never stood up to him. Didn't she ever want to, Lissa wondered? Didn't she ever want to yell at him the way he yelled at them? Didn't she ever want to have a bad day and take it out on him?

Obviously Lissa must be the one who was mistaken. When her mother looked at her father, all Lissa saw was love. She seemed to adore him no matter what he said or did. She never complained, never cried, never escaped.

How did she do it? Lissa would go crazy without her books and her secret drawings and her dreams as she lay in her canopy bed. She would go crazy if she didn't get out of this house to go to school, even if she was almost as quiet there as she was here.

At least at school, the teachers seemed to think she was close enough to perfect to be acceptable. If she could get out of high school, then she could go to college. She could go *away* to college. Her father was selling more and more paintings so they must have enough money to send her. She knew she would miss her mother tremendously, but she also knew that a fresh start, a distance from this life, would set her free. Nobody would know who she was. Nobody would know whose daughter she was.

The newspaper writer came a few days later. She was an attractive woman with long red nails and black hair, and she actually got to go into the barn. Lissa was amazed. Even her mother wasn't allowed to do that. Eventually the writer and her father came into the house and sat in the living room. She was laughing, and her voice sounded excited and interested. Lissa's father was actually laughing, too. Lissa and her mother sat in the kitchen, almost afraid to breathe. Lissa kept wondering when the mood would change, when her father would start to yell.

As the writer was leaving, she came through the kitchen and spoke to Lissa's mother. Lissa had walked outside, but she could hear their voices.

"It must be exciting to live with such a talented, charming man," the writer said with almost a sigh.

Charming?

"I feel fortunate to be part of his life," Lissa's mother said. "He works very hard, and it's important that he have a quiet, calm environment in which to restore his energies."

"Still," the woman said, "you're in the shadow of genius."

Lissa didn't like that thought. She didn't like the thought of her mother being in shadow. She wanted to think of her in the bright sunlight, enjoying her flowers.

Besides, if her mother was in the shadows, where was she?

She remembered reading the article when it came out a week or so later. Two things stuck in her memory forever from that article.

The first was a quote from her father: "I need complete isolation to exercise my creativity. I love to be alone."

The second was a simple fact. Although the article talked about her mother and her role in supporting the proper environment for her father's painting, there was no mention at all that he had a daughter. None. It was as if Lissa didn't exist.

The day after the article came out, right about dinnertime, a car pulled up the driveway and stopped in front of the house. Lissa remembered being startled because they never had visitors. She and her mother went out, and a girl that Lissa vaguely recognized from school got out, followed by a woman that Lissa supposed was the girl's mother.

"Hello," the woman said in a voice so cheerful that it was sickening. "I'm just so excited. So excited. This is my daughter Nicollette. She's a friend of your daughter's from school."

A friend? Lissa had never exchanged a word with the girl. She was at least a grade ahead of her, and she traveled in social circles of which Lissa was definitely no part: the girls who dressed perfectly, laughed perfectly, and got the attention of all the boys who played sports perfectly, got in trouble perfectly, and didn't spend a single second looking at a quiet little mouse like Lissa.

"Well, my Nicollette wants to be an artist. In fact, I have some of her work right here, and it would mean the world, just the world to her if she could speak to your husband for a moment, just a teensy moment. I'm sure that he could tell her just what to do."

Lissa looked at Nicollette. At least she looked just a little bit embarrassed, although that didn't ruffle her perfect long blonde hair or bring a flush to her perfectly pink cheeks.

"I don't think that will be possible," Lissa's mother said politely. "My husband is still working, and he doesn't like to be disturbed."

"Maybe Nicollette could just watch him, then," the woman persisted. "She'd be quiet as can be. He wouldn't even know she was there. I'm sure she could learn a lot just by being near him."

Who did this woman think she was? Lissa had lived here for her entire life, and other than a quick peek through the window, she'd never watched her father work.

Then her heart rate picked up significantly. She heard the slam of the barn door and saw her father approach across the yard. His steps were fast, his face crossed with a frown. This was not going to be good.

Lissa's mother must have felt the same way. "This might not be a good time," she said quickly. "Perhaps you'd better leave."

"Oh look, Nicollette," the woman squealed. "It's him! He's right here! Go talk to him!"

Nicollette didn't move, but she flashed a brilliant smile toward Lissa's father. Lissa fully expected him to veer off and head for the back door, and he almost did, but then he looked at the two visitors and headed their way. Great, Lissa thought. This should trigger a fine explosion.

As soon as Lissa's father was within earshot, the woman began babbling about her daughter. Her father, much to her amazement, came up to them. Totally ignoring her mother, her, and the woman, he focused on Nicollette. "You do *not* want to be an artist," he said, his voice gravelly. "On days when nothing goes well, there is no more miserable existence."

"But on days when it goes well, there must be nothing more wonderful," Nicollette said, her voice sweet.

"True," he said, "but those days are rare."

"I'm willing to work very, very hard to be a good artist," Nicollette said earnestly. "I'd give anything in the world to be like you."

Lissa waited for her father to laugh in Nicolette's face, but he didn't.

Suddenly the woman, who had been watching this with eyes big, mouth open in a wide O, snapped back to life. "Look at these," she said, shoving a large manila folder at Lissa's father. "This is my daughter's artwork. I'm sure she has a lot of talent."

"Mother," Nicollette said, shaking her head.

"It's all right," Lissa's father said to Nicollette. He opened the folder and looked at the first drawing. Lissa could see over his shoulder, and she waited to hear his snort of disgust. The drawing was of a unicorn with clouds overhead and a garland of flowers circling its neck. The unicorn had huge eyes with long lashes. Please. She knew how much her father hated that fantasy stuff.

He turned to the next picture. It was a sketch of a Raggedy Ann doll done in colored pencil. The next one was a badly smudged pastel chalk picture of a clown. The last one was a sketch of a face.

"That's me," the woman announced proudly. "Didn't she just capture me?"

Lissa never would have known the identity of the subject had the woman not announced

The *Point Horror* Club...

We Dare You!

All for only £3.95* Introductory offer worth over £12*

The Point Horror Club, the place to get hooked on horror with frightening books and your mirror spy sunglasses. Start your own collection and prepare to be scared. Your introductory pack will arrive at your house in about two weeks, then, with no obligation and for as long as you want we will send you another scary pack each month. Each new pack contains 3 horror titles and will cost you only £6.99, saving pounds on the normal prices. You can cancel at any time. Return the coupon with your Parent's/Guardian's signature with only £3.95*... if you dare!

*Inc VAT

PLUS Mirror Spy Glasses – see who's creeping up behind you...

Don't call for help, he may just kill you.

THE LIFEGUARD
Richie Tankersley Cusick

He has been dead for thousands of years... but he can't rest, alone.

THE MUMMY
Barbara Steiner
He can't rest easy... alone.

Point Horror
APRIL FOOLS
Richie Tankersley Cusick
If it's no joke... it's murder.

April Fool's day is over, but it's no joke... it's murder.

POINT HORROR CLUB ORDER FORM

Yes! I dare you to scare me! Please send me my introductory Point Horror Pack for just £3.95*. *Please make payable to Scholastic Ltd.*

Please return to Scholastic Book Clubs, FREEPOST CV3066, Westfield Road, Southam, Leamington Spa, Warwickshire CV33 0BR.

THIS SECTION MUST BE COMPLETED BY A PARENT / GUARDIAN

Parent's / Guardian's Name

Address

Post Code

Signature _____ I am over 18.

Offer valid only in the UK and the Republic of Ireland. If you are not entirely delighted with your introductory offer you can return it for a full refund.

SCHOLASTIC

12919-4

it. The face on the paper bore no resemblance at all to the woman.

Lissa almost felt sorry for Nicollette. It wouldn't be easy to hear what her father was going to say. Still, she had brought it on herself by allowing her mother to drag her to their house.

"You definitely show talent," her father said to Nicollette, handing her the folder. "You're willing to use a variety of media, and you're finding your strengths. The art world needs a wide range of styles, and I'm sure that you can find your own niche. Keep drawing. It's a skill that has to be practiced and honed."

"Thank you," Nicollette said gravely. "That means a great deal to me coming from you."

"You're a charming young lady," her father said. "Pleased to meet you. If I may be of help, let me know. Now I need to be going." With a final smile to Nicollette and no acknowledgement of the rest of them, he went into the house.

Behind her, Lissa could hear her mother let out her breath in relief.

"See, I knew it would be fine if we stopped by," the woman said to her mother, smiling smugly. "And you thought we'd be bothering him."

"There's just no anticipating his moods," her mother said evenly.

The woman and Nicollette walked toward their car. "I'm sure you two girls will see each other in school," the woman called back.

Sure. As they passed in the hallways with no acknowledgement of each other, Lissa thought.

Her mother rushed into the house to finish dinner, and Lissa sat down on the step, her head spinning, her stomach knotted.

Nicollette was a charming young lady, according to her father. She was also, near as Lissa could tell, her exact opposite. She was tall where Lissa was short. She had long blonde hair where hers was dark and cropped short. Nicollette was confident and polished where she was too shy to even speak to others. She was popular where Lissa was a nobody.

She had talent, but her father had mocked the one drawing of Lissa's that he had ever seen.

She had talent?

If Nicollette was what her father wanted in a daughter, then she was doomed. There was no way that he would ever love her.

Lissa thought that was the day that she started to give up hoping that her father would ever love her.

Chapter 8

Lissa had come to know that her father did not love her. It took her a long time, though, to find the courage to ask her mother why she loved him.

It puzzled her. He seemed so cold, so distant to her. Her mother seemed to function as his servant more than as his equal, his love. Why did she put up with him? Why did she remain so unfailingly supportive, calm, and patient in the face of his constant bad moods and demands?

Lissa didn't have a choice, but she did. Why did her mother love him?

Lissa finally asked her one day when her father had been particularly difficult. Everything bothered him: dinner, her mother's attempts at conversation, Lissa's silence, the fact that it was warm outside. When he announced that he was going back to the barn to waste more time on a painting that would never turn out right — a statement that he made about every painting at some point during its creation — her mother decided to take Lissa into town for an ice cream cone. There was a store with homemade mint chocolate chip ice cream that they both loved, and her mother seemed to save it for times when her father had been particularly difficult.

Lissa's mother had barely been breathing, it seemed, until her father was once again behind the slammed barn door, and they were driving out of their road and onto the paved road to town. She expelled her breath in a sigh of relief, it seemed to Lissa. Although it was not like her to speak frankly to anyone, even to her mother, the tension of the scene at dinner had done more than what it usually did, which was to make her feel sad and guilty. This time it also made Lissa a little angry. From that anger came her question.

"Why do you put up with him?" Even though her voice was soft, it was quivering with emotion.

"Lissa, why would you ever ask that?" Her mother's eyes left the road to look at her in puzzlement.

"He's mean to you."

"He doesn't intend to be," her mother

quickly answered. "It's just that he's very temperamental, very high-strung. You know how it is with these creative, artistic types."

"But you're not that way," she said.

"That's because I'm neither creative nor artistic," her mother said with a smile.

"But he's always snapping at you, criticizing everything. Don't you want to just yell back?"

"What would that accomplish?" her mother asked sincerely. "He'd just get more tense, and we don't need that, do we?"

"No," Lissa admitted. "I just don't see how you stand it."

"Your father can also be very charming when he wants to be," her mother said after a pause.

When does he ever want to be? Lissa asked herself. To people at gallery shows? To Nicollette? When is he ever charming to us?

She guessed her mother picked up her silence. "Lissa, your father is a very difficult man. I know that he is sometimes very remote, and he isn't like the fathers you read about in books or see on television. It's just that he lives in his head. He's seeing visions of things he wants to paint, and sometimes I think those visions are more real to him than real life. It doesn't mean that he doesn't love us."

Love us? Lissa thought. Love you. That might be the question. I know that he doesn't love me. Still, she couldn't say those words out loud to her mother. She knew they would hurt her.

Lissa realized suddenly that she knew nothing about the early days of her mother and father. Maybe that would help her to understand. "How did you meet him?" she asked.

"Why the sudden curiosity?" her mother asked, but she didn't sound offended.

"I don't know," Lissa said. "I just realized that I don't know anything about how you met."

"It's not a very exciting story," her mother said. "I'm afraid you'll be disappointed. Still, if you want to know, there's no reason why you shouldn't."

"Tell me," she said. Maybe she would understand more.

"We met when I was a junior in college," her mother began. "I was a computer science major, and I had one group requirement left in the humanities. I'd put it off for as long as I could since I knew that my strengths were in the logical areas, not the creative ones. I was good in math and science and computers, but I dreaded the thought of interpreting literature or appreciating music or any of those other humanities electives. Anyway, one of my friends had taken an introduction to art class with a young teaching assistant. She claimed to have no artistic talent whatsoever, but she said that the teaching assistant graded purely on effort, and the class was a breeze. That was all I needed to hear. I even double-checked with her to make sure that I signed up for the right section."

Lissa was listening to this with great interest. She hadn't even known that her mother had majored in computer science. She had never mentioned her college days to her.

"Anyway, I walked in the first day of class, ready to draw trees or whatever I'd have to do to get through. Imagine my surprise, however, when this intense, glowering man introduced himself. He said that the regular teaching assistant had become ill, and that he would be taking over our class for the semester. He made it perfectly clear that he normally only taught upper-level art majors and that he was insulted by having to deal with such rank amateurs, but he'd have to endure it."

"And that was my father?" she asked.

"That was my first introduction to him," her mother said with a smile. "As soon as my friend heard who I had for art class, she told me to drop the class immediately. She said that she'd heard stories about him all over campus. Evidently he wasn't satisfied until he'd torn students' work apart so thoroughly that they ran out crying."

"Why didn't you drop the class?" Lissa asked.

"There was nothing else available that would fit in my schedule, and I figured, how bad could it really be? It was only three hours a week for one semester."

"Was it bad?" she asked.

"It was dreadful," her mother said, but she laughed as she said it. "He started out giving us these complicated drawings to do, and none of us could do them to his satisfaction. He said that my still life of pears looked like roadkill on the expressway."

"That's mean. You weren't an art major. You were trying your best."

"But it *did* look like roadkill," her mother said with a laugh. "You can't believe how terrible I was. There were some people in the class who actually had some talent, but I wasn't one of them. I couldn't see angles or shapes or perspective, and I had no sense of color or shading or anything. I was hopeless."

"So he yelled at you all the time?"

"Yes, he yelled. And at first it upset me. I

mean, I was used to getting good grades and getting along with my professors, and here he was using my work as the perfect example of everything that could be done wrong."

"But you still didn't drop the class?"

"Just about when I was ready to, figuring that I was going to fail anyway, something changed. I don't know if I changed or if he changed, but suddenly it became funny. I still tried to do things right, and he still yelled, but somehow that became what the class looked forward to. I was the comic relief that got the rest of them off the hook. Compared to me, the rest of them looked good. When they heard that I was thinking of dropping, they begged me to stay. It really *was* funny, Lissa."

She had to admit that she could see the humor even though she couldn't imagine being the class failure.

"Eventually your father and I came to an understanding. I promised him that I was fully planning to stay a computer science major and that I would never take another art class or ever admit to anybody that he had been my teacher. In exchange, he backed off a little on the criticism and actually tried to help me see things like an artist."

Her mother stopped like this was the end

of the story. Really, though, it was only the start of what Lissa wanted to know. "Then what happened?" she prodded.

"You know, nobody was more surprised than I was when he tracked me down on campus a week or so after my class with him ended. He said that he missed seeing his absolute opposite."

"You *are* opposites," Lissa said.

"We are in many ways," her mother agreed. "He knew that he was impatient and rude with people and totally out of touch with the daily routines of living. You should have seen his apartment when he was teaching. The first time I went there, I almost died. There were clothes and painting supplies and dirty dishes and unopened mail thrown everywhere. He had no food, at least not any that wasn't growing mold. He couldn't find anything, not even his telephone."

"So you cleaned it all up," Lissa said, starting to envision her mother, young and awed by the crazy artist.

"How did you know?" her mother said with a smile. "Before either of us realized it, I was shopping for his food, keeping his apartment in order, eventually even coding in his grade sheets and making sure he met the college's deadlines."

"So you took care of him," Lissa said.

"It didn't feel like that, though," her mother said a little defensively. "It was fun. It was like playing house or something. And for a long time there was nothing romantic. He was a lot older than me, and I didn't think he'd ever be interested in anybody as ordinary as me."

"Why would you feel that way?" she asked her.

"Because that was the truth," her mother stated simply. "I got good grades, but I wasn't exceptionally brilliant or talented. I got by on a lot of hard work. I was on the shy side, and I kept to myself a lot of the time. If I did make myself go to a party, I was most likely the one who sat in the corner all night, watching everybody else. Your father, on the other hand, was already building a reputation as an artist. Everybody knew it would just be a matter of time before he left teaching to paint full time. And talk about attractive. Half of the girls who weren't running away from him in tears were in love with him. He was so critical that if he ever said anything even halfway nice to them, they thought they'd won some huge prize. All he had to do was walk into a room and all eyes were on him. You may not realize it, Lissa, but your father is a very charismatic man."

If she thought about him as if he were a

stranger, she guessed he was attractive. He had thick, curly gray hair that sort of reminded her of a lion's mane, and he was thin, always wearing the same jeans and oversized shirt. She guessed that he was dramatic, unlike some fathers who wore boring navy suits to work every day.

"Then what happened?" she asked, wanting to hear the rest of the story.

"Then that second semester finished, and I went home for the summer to work for a bank that had hired me for the past several summers. I didn't guess he'd even think about me, and I didn't hear a word from him all summer. When I went back to college to start my senior year, though, I ran into him on campus the very first day. He took me back to his apartment, which was a total wreck again, and he said that he had missed me. I thought he meant that he missed all the work I did for him, and I jokingly told him that he'd better hire a maid. He got mad at that, though, and said that he had spent time that summer thinking, and that he cared about me more than he had realized."

And she fell for that? Lissa thought. Then she shook her head at her own negativity. Why was she being so cynical?

"So then our relationship changed. We never actually dated, but we began to spend a lot of time together, and by the time my senior year ended, it somehow had become agreed upon between us that we would get married."

"Did he propose to you?"

"No," her mother said. "It was more like we just eventually assumed that we'd stay together. I don't know how to explain it. I always knew that he didn't want any big ceremony, that we'd just go to the justice of the peace and do the formalities."

"So you didn't have a wedding or anything?"

"Sorry to disappoint you, but we didn't. I graduated, we got married, he quit teaching, and we moved here. It was quite a risk at the start, but he had some money saved, and we both believed that his paintings would sell."

"And so this became your life?" Lissa asked.

"Yes, Lissa, this became my life," her mother said, and Lissa thought she sounded a little angry at her wording. "You have to understand. I don't feel like I have any significant talent to contribute to the world. What gives me satisfaction is knowing that I am making it easier for someone who does have a great talent to lead a productive life. He has the talent to create the masterpieces; I am capable of taking care of all the everyday details that allow him to work."

"So you're content to always be behind the scenes?" Lissa asked, despite her fear that again her mother wouldn't like her question.

"Yes, Lissa, I am. I have no desire to be in the spotlight. I'd rather be backstage, out of the glare, or else out in the audience applauding. That's my role, and I accepted that a long time ago."

She thought her mother was being too hard on herself. When had she ever really had a chance to shine for herself? She had gone straight from college to life in her husband's shadow. Still, Lissa understood more than she had before. Her mother felt a part of Lissa's father's success, even though he never seemed to give her any credit for it.

Still, where did that leave Lissa? What was her role in all of this? It seemed like she had nothing to offer to her father, nothing at all.

She wondered if he had wanted her. She wondered if he had been happy that she was conceived and born.

Somehow she thought she knew the answers to those questions, but she was afraid to ask and hear the answers out loud.

Chapter 9

This was not what Lissa had in mind. This searching of memory was only making her sadder, and it was not granting her any peace of mind. She had known these pieces for years. Why weren't they fitting together in any new order?

It seemed to her that knowing she was near dying should bring her a clarity, an insight that would allow her to understand. After all, it was her last chance.

She shifted her body slightly then regretted the movement. Her body was becoming numb, and disturbing it brought unwelcome flashes of pain from nerve endings she'd rather not feel. At least Bird had once again settled into sleep. She could feel his tiny heart beating, its rapid pace sustaining that fierce spark of life. He had a feisty spirit for such a small creature.

He had amazed her from the first day he came home with her.

No, she wasn't ready to think about that day. Not yet. She frantically searched for a different memory, any memory, to shove that one aside for at least a little bit longer.

Josh. She had sworn that she wouldn't remember him, but his face swam before her eyes, full of smiling vitality. She had never met a person in her life who had Josh's joy about each day, each moment. Everything was an adventure to him, a romp. He was so different from Lissa that it seemed they were different species, creatures from different planets. She was from a place that was often dark, or at least shrouded in mist and clouds. Josh was pure light. Lissa had read once that people have auras of light that surround them. If that was true, then her aura was a dark, cloudy blue, and Josh's was yellow and vibrant like the sun.

She remembered the day that the generator blew up at school. It was maybe a few weeks after Josh had given her the flowers and card, and in between they had had some brief conversations, before or after English class or when he found her in the hallway and spun in circles around her, laughing and teasing and begging her to smile. Then one day in the middle of class, the lights went out. Several girls screamed, which struck Lissa as stupid since there was still light coming in the windows. Josh, sitting behind her like always, put both hands on her shoulders and proclaimed, in a booming, heroic voice, "Don't worry, Lissa. I'll save you. We'll find a way to get out alive." That broke the tension in the room, and everybody laughed.

Then the fire alarm began to ring, and again a few people seemed willing to panic, more for effect than from necessity. As kids crammed through the doorway, Josh waited beside Lissa while she gathered her books and waited for the bedlam to quiet a little. Still, even she got a little nervous when smoke began to filter into the hallways. Every school has monthly fire drills, but this was obviously something out of the ordinary.

Josh grabbed on to the strap of her bookbag, making certain that they didn't get separated in the crowd that was now pushing and shoving toward the stairwells and exits. They moved with the flow of humanity, smoke stinging their eyes, until they made it outside. Administrators and teachers were yelling for everybody to go sit in the bleachers in the football stadium, and the distant sound of fire engine sirens could already be heard.

Josh and Lissa went to the stadium, staying on the ground near the ramp, watching people scream and shout and fool around once they were sure that they were safe. A cloud of smoke was hanging over part of the school's roof, and a group of teachers were arguing fiercely with a cluster of students who claimed that they had to go back in to get their belongings.

Finally the principal brought a bullhorn to the stadium, and after about five minutes of screaming for attention, got enough silence to be heard. He announced that there was a fire in one of the electrical generators on the roof, that the fire was contained and would not damage the building, but that the fire marshall did not want anybody to go back inside until fans could pull out the smoke. Therefore, school was dismissed for the day. After the cheering had quieted, he announced that those who drove were free to leave, and that those who rode buses needed to wait in the stadium for approximately the next hour, which was how long it would take to get the buses back.

"Let's go," Josh said as soon as the principal finished. It seemed like everybody had suddenly driven to school because the bleachers were emptying rapidly.

"I ride a bus," Lissa said. "I'll have to wait here."

"I'll drive you home," Josh said.

"No," she said quickly, too quickly and too sharply. Josh looked at her curiously. What made it worse was that she couldn't explain. She couldn't tell him that nobody could know where she lived.

"Really, it's no problem," Josh said.

Lissa shook her head silently. The risk was too great. Nobody had visited where she now lived. Nobody.

"Okay, then let's go walk around until your bus comes," Josh said, still looking confused and almost hurt.

She followed behind him as he strode off. She didn't want to draw any more attention to her refusal by making yet another one. They walked in silence, which was unusual for Josh. Lissa guessed he was trying to figure out why she was being so weird. Unfortunately, she couldn't help him.

About three blocks away from the school there was a small park. Lissa had gone past it, but she had never been in it. There was a small playground for children, and then a wooded area that was dotted with picnic tables. On the far side there were two tennis courts. Almost as if he knew, almost as if he could read her mind, Josh headed straight for the swings.

She hadn't been on swings since elementary school, but the sensation immediately came back to her. She pushed off strongly, pumping her legs, leaning back until her body was extended in a straight line. Josh was flying right beside her. She kept on and on and on until her legs finally tired. Then she leaned back, letting the momentum finally die away.

"I don't believe it," Josh said when he had stopped beside her. "I absolutely don't believe it."

"What?" she asked quietly.

"You're smiling," he said, staring at her face. "Wait. Let me memorize this moment. Princess Lissa is smiling."

Of course, his attention immediately made her stop smiling. "I had forgotten how much I loved to swing," she said finally.

"Did you ever go over the top bar?" Josh asked, scuffing his sneakers in the dirt.

"No. Did you?"

"Nope, but it was always my goal. The bigger boys claimed that if you went high enough, you could make a complete circle all the way over the top. I'd hate to think how many hours I spent trying to do that."

"I always wanted to fly away," Lissa said, remembering. "I always wanted to fly away to the tops of the trees and live there."

"You still do, don't you?" Josh asked, his voice suddenly gentle. "You'd rather be anywhere other than where you are, wouldn't you?"

"You mean here with you?" Lissa asked.

"No, I just mean here in general. I watch you in school, and you always seem a million miles away."

Lissa knew she needed to say something in the resulting silence. "I don't seem to fit in very well," she said cautiously.

"Well, thank heavens for that," Josh said, breaking the quiet mood and bounding off the swing. "I couldn't stand one more giggly, noisy girl. Besides, you're a challenge. If I make you smile, that's really an accomplishment. Come on. I know a place you'll love."

She followed him. He led her to what seemed to be the biggest tree in the park. "Come on up," he said, swinging himself on to a low branch, then immediately climbing higher.

Lissa looked at him in amazement. She couldn't do that.

"Trust me, Lissa. This is the best climbing tree in the park. I used to do it all the time, even when I was seven or eight. You can do it. Grab the low branch and pull yourself up. The rest is easy. I'll tell you where to put your feet."

Trust him? When had she ever been able to trust? She looked up at the huge tree, frightened. Still, the upper branches seemed to beckon her.

Josh shinnied down until he was only one branch up from the first one. "Come on, Lissa. I won't let you fall. Get up on the first branch."

Dubiously, she shrugged off her bookbag, leaving it against the trunk of the tree. She stretched her hands up until they barely gripped the rough bark of the branch. Her hands were too small to circle the branch, and she couldn't get a firm grip.

"Brace your feet against the trunk and push up," Josh encouraged. "Here. As soon as you get part way up, I'll grab your right hand."

She followed his instructions, barely making any progress, but Josh was as good as his word and grabbed her wrist firmly with his hand, hauling her unceremoniously to the first branch. Once she got to her feet, hugging the trunk for balance, it was easier. The branches made almost a staircase up, and with Josh grabbing on to her with every move, telling her not to look down, she was soon about twenty feet up into the tree.

"Here's the best sitting branch," Josh said, guiding her so that she sat on a huge branch, nestled against the trunk for security. "Wait until I'm settled beside you, and then you can look."

Lissa waited until she felt him sit beside her, and then she looked down. After the first mild wave of dizziness, she was amazed at how high up they were. Then she looked out through the leaves. It was wonderful. It was as if they were in their own world, up above the normal, everyday world. She could see into the tops of neighboring trees and out onto the rest of the park.

"Stay very quiet," Josh whispered. "The birds will come."

After a few motionless minutes, he was right. Several different little birds, sparrows maybe, started to return to nearby branches, eyeing them curiously. Lissa was afraid to move a muscle, not wanting to scare them away, wanting to be accepted as a part of their world.

Josh was the one who eventually broke the spell. "I knew you'd like it here," he said quietly.

"It's wonderful," she said.

"I've been climbing this tree for years," Josh said. "Once my mother about killed me because she was looking all over the park for me, and I was up in the tree, watching her hunt. At the time, it struck me as hilariously funny."

"Do you still come here often?" Lissa asked.

"Not so much any more," Josh said. "Sometimes when I really need to think, I come here late at night and climb up and look at the stars and clear my mind."

"That must be peaceful," she said.

"If you ever need to come here, just tell me," Josh said. "I'll bring you here, any time of the day or night."

Lissa was moved by his genuine kindness. She didn't understand why he was extending it, but it touched her. "Thank you," she said seriously. She wanted to say more, but she couldn't.

"But you won't ask, will you, mysterious Princess Lissa? You won't let anybody across the drawbridge and over the moat."

"It's not that simple," she said, knowing that this conversation was heading in a dangerous direction. "Look." She pointed off toward the school parking lot, visible from their perch. "Here come the buses."

"As you wish," Josh said, flashing a smile,

even though it wasn't the brilliant one that usually adorned his face. "I'll help you down."

Lissa retrieved her bookbag, suddenly feeling weighted down again. They walked back to school, and Josh repeated his offer to take her home. She told him her bus was right there, and that she'd see him tomorrow in English.

"Thank you for the swings. Thank you for the tree," she said as she boarded the steps of the glaring yellow bus.

"Thank you for the smile," Josh said, then turned to bound rapidly away.

Chapter 10

Despite everything, the memory of Josh's kindness brought a slight smile to Lissa's face. That was wiped away quickly, however, by the return of the footsteps. They were a distance away, but they seemed to be more systematic, moving first in one direction, then in the other. Would the sweep bring the footsteps right to her nest under the roots of the big tree?

Probably.

No, definitely.

She was being stalked, hunted, and the woods were not big enough or deep enough or dense enough to hide her forever.

She would be found. Then she would die.

It was time now. She had to go to the worst parts. Perhaps the pain would give her the answers she sought. Besides, what were the memories of pain compared to the death that she faced? Soon she would feel no more pain, no more fear, no more betrayal.

Soon she would feel nothing.

Her right leg twitched slightly as if in memory of its injury. Some hurts could heal; others remained always.

She had been a junior in high school. She remembered that specifically because she was nearing the end of the school year, and she was anticipating only one more year of high school. She had skipped a grade in elementary school and would graduate at seventeen. Then college. Then freedom.

The year had gone well academically; once again Lissa had earned all A's, and she had even enjoyed some of her classes. To be sure, she didn't participate voluntarily or outwardly show her enthusiasm, but inside her mind she appreciated the skills of her teachers, the interesting insights of the books she read and the history she studied. Even math had a certain pure beauty to it — logical, rational, clean.

Her mind on her upcoming final exams, going through her plan for studying that night, Lissa had been distracted at the dinner table. She rarely spoke at dinner, only responding to direct questions from her mother, but she usually kept track of the conversation between her mother and her father. It was highly predictable: complaints from her father about how poorly his painting was going, followed by reassurances from her mother that he would conquer any difficulties, just as he always did.

That particular evening, though, that pleasant late May evening when her mind was on math review and the best way to memorize the significant dates in a year's worth of history study, she didn't hear her father speak to her.

"Lissa. Lissa!" she heard her mother say urgently.

Lissa turned to face her mother, jerking back to reality. "Yes?" she asked.

"Your father . . ." her mother began.

"Don't I deserve the courtesy of a simple answer to a simple question?" her father snapped.

"I'm sorry," Lissa said quickly. "What did you ask?"

"I'm not going to repeat myself for you," her father said, voice rising angrily.

"Fine," Lissa had said evenly. Before she could say the next words, which were "I apologize for not paying attention," her father had launched out of his chair and was standing over her.

"I don't kill myself earning the money to pay for your upkeep to be smart-mouthed by you," he yelled. "Get out of my sight."

Gladly, Lissa thought, but had the wisdom not to say. She glanced briefly at her mother, who seemed frozen, then pushed away from the table and moved quickly across the room to the steps that led to the second floor and her bedroom. She could still hear her father ranting angrily when she reached the haven of her bedroom, giving the door a yank behind her to make certain that it closed.

To this day, Lissa did not believe that she meant to slam the door. Yes, she had meant for it to shut, but she hadn't meant for it to slam. Maybe there was some angry, repressed part of her mind that wanted the satisfaction of noise, but she wasn't aware of it.

She actually wasn't aware of much except relief at being away from her father when she heard the stomping footsteps pound up the stairs. Her bedroom door crashed open to reveal the furious face of her father.

"Who do you think you are?" he bellowed. "Who do you think you are to slam doors in my house? I won't have it. I will not have it."

Lissa stared at him in amazement. She was used to being ignored, not to being the focus of his rage.

"You will march yourself downstairs right

this minute, come up these stairs and close that door in an acceptable manner. Do you understand?"

Lissa nodded silently but didn't move, unsure of whether motion would appease or anger him.

"I said now," her father hissed, and he grabbed her arm and yanked.

Lissa stared down at his hand on her arm as if she were looking at something strange and alien, something separate from her body. Her father never touched her. He never hugged her or patted her shoulder or took her hand; he also never touched her in anger. Through her bewilderment, pain began to register as his fingers tightened.

"Now," he said, his voice more frightening quiet than it had been loud. He yanked on her arm, pulling her back toward the steps.

She wanted to tell him that she would do what he wanted, that she would go downstairs and come back up and shut the door properly. She would do whatever it took to get away from him. The words, however, were bottled up inside of her. She could not force them past the lump in her throat.

He pulled her violently to the top of the steps and started down. Later, Lissa wasn't certain what made her lose her balance. It might have been her father's abrupt motion, or it might have been her sandal catching an edge of the small rug at the top of the steps. It might have been a combination of both.

It didn't really matter. Lissa remembered her fall down that flight of steps as if it happened in slow motion. They were hardwood, uncarpeted, and she pitched over as she fell, hitting her head, then her back, as she catapulted to the bottom. She was stunned, too taken aback to even register pain, until she hit the bottom.

It was, she guessed, the perfectly wrong combination of momentum and angle. Her leg was twisted under her as she landed in an awkward bend, and she heard, clearly, distinctly, unmistakably, the crack of the bone.

Then her leg went numb. She didn't know how long it was before her father brushed past her as she lay crumpled on the floor, how long before she looked up into the anguished face of her mother rushing out from the kitchen.

"Get up," her father had said, but there was a note of hesitation in his voice.

"My leg is broken," she said softly, with certainty. That was all that she had said.

Lissa remembered her mother crying out, and she remembered hearing the slamming of the door as her father left. She remembered the agonizing pain that shot through her leg, reawakening it, as her mother helped her up, supporting her as she made her way to the car, where she somehow got into the back-seat.

Lissa remembered wishing that her mother would call an ambulance so she wouldn't have to move on her own, but she never mentioned that. She had only known that she wanted out of that house, and that she wanted the pain to back off so that she could get a grip on it. She only knew that she didn't want to think about this. She wanted to wake up and discover that it was all a nightmare, a terrible mistake played on her by an overactive imagination.

But it wasn't a dream. Her mother had taken her to the emergency room of the nearest hospital. As the attendants approached, her mother had leaned back to her over the front seat, and had spoken to her for the first time other than her reassurances that they were almost there and that it would be all right.

"Please tell them that you just fell. Tell them that it was an accident, Lissa. Your father didn't mean it. He didn't mean to hurt you. Please don't mention him."

Lissa had never answered her. She tried to sort out the truth through the haze of pain. If it wasn't her father's fault, then it must be hers. She must have deserved it. Still, the memory of his hand was imprinted on her arm. Curious, Lissa looked down at her arm. The distinct fingerprints of bruises were already clear on her flesh.

Her mother's eyes followed the path that Lissa's took. "Here," she said, quickly pulling off the light sweater that she was wearing over her shirt. "Put this on. You're shaking. You must be cold."

Lissa had turned her face away as her mother slowly put the sweater on her.

The blessed relief of painkillers followed a series of x-rays that confirmed a clean break. Her leg had been encased in an unwieldy plaster cast, and she drifted in and out of a drugged sleep. Only one nurse asked her how it happened, and she seemed easily satisfied with the statement that Lissa had tripped and fallen down the steps at home.

It was, after all, the truth. At least it was part of the truth.

When she and her mother had gotten home late that night, the house was completely dark. Lights shone from the barn.

After her mother helped her up the steps, awkward with the cast, and settled Lissa into bed, she stroked her short hair, but she couldn't seem to meet her daughter's eyes.

"I'm sorry, Lissa," she finally said. "I'm sorry this happened to you. You did the right thing, though."

Lissa had turned to face the wall, wanting her mother to leave her alone.

She had slept off and on, tormented by nightmares, tormented by thoughts.

Chapter 11

Lissa hated thinking about her leg because that had been the start of the really bad stuff. Still, one good thing had come out of that experience. That was what had allowed her to get Bird.

Several days after the fall, her leg still painful, her body still adjusting to the awkwardness of the cast, Lissa had awakened after a restless night.

It was her birthday. She was sixteen. Somehow it didn't seem right. Instead of that being a milestone, a reason for celebration, her birthday seemed like just another day, and a not very pleasant one at that. It was Saturday. She had not yet gone back to school, and exams would be starting soon. The house was even more tense than usual. Her father now stayed in the barn through dinner, not coming in until hours later. When he did, he did not even look at Lissa. She could see the strain in her mother's face, the tension in her mouth, the dull look of apprehension in her eyes.

Although Lissa would welcome the end of the school year and the finishing of the frantic studying, in some ways she was sad. At least school was a place to hear laughter. Granted it was other people's laughter, not her own, but it wasn't a sound she was likely to hear at home.

Happy birthday, Lissa, she thought to herself. She figured she'd maneuver down the steps to get something for breakfast, then treat herself to a few hours of reading the latest John Irving novel before she began to study.

Her mother, however, had different plans. "Happy birthday, Lissa," she said with frantic cheerfulness when Lissa appeared in the kitchen. "I made you French toast with fresh strawberries and whipped cream. Then we're going to go shopping for your birthday present." She hesitated awkwardly. "Your father is working already, but he wanted me to wish you a happy birthday, too."

Sure, Lissa thought. First he totally ignores me, and then he wishes me a happy birthday? Somehow it didn't fit. Besides, she would have staked her life on the fact that her father had completely forgotten. Why would he remember the birthday of a daughter that he couldn't even stand to be in the same room with?

Lissa opened the birthday card that was beside her plate. Happy birthday to a wonderful daughter. Love, Mother and Dad.

Yes, but the Mother and Dad were both written in her mother's handwriting.

"I thought that now that you are sixteen, you'd like to pick out your own present," her mother said as Lissa ate. "Whatever you want, whatever will make you happy. Up to the limit on my charge card, at least."

"I really don't need anything," Lissa said, not liking what she heard in her mother's voice. Was it guilt?

"Then we'll get you something you want if you don't need anything. I insist."

"It's just so awkward to get around," Lissa said, feeling uncomfortable about the thought of going out in public. She was still unsteady on the crutches the doctor had given her.

"You'll do fine. Besides, it's good practice if you're going back to school on Monday."

"I have to go back because of exams," Lissa reminded her.

"I know," her mother said. "But let's not think about that today. You're sixteen, and we're going to buy you the perfect present."

Lissa had given in, and an hour later they were at the mall. It had seemed like the greatest number of shopping options with the least amount of walking. Lissa figured she'd find a dress or some pants or something, tell her mother she loved them, and that would do it. Truly, she didn't care. There was no gift that excited her.

They looked through the clothes in the large department store that anchored one corner of the mall, then went into several smaller clothing stores nearby. Lissa couldn't even find anything to pretend to like. She couldn't try on pants with the cast, and even trying on a dress would require more of a balancing act than she wanted to attempt.

Her mother could see her lack of enthusiasm. "I know," she said. "Let's look at jewelry. That would be the perfect sixteenth birthday present. It would be something you could always keep to remind you of being sweet sixteen."

Somehow Lissa didn't think she wanted a permanent reminder of this birthday, but she went along. They went into a jewelry store partway down the major stretch of the mall, and her mother immediately gravitated toward the pearls. She asked to see a short strand,

and she caressed the milky beads. Lissa watched.

"What do you think?" her mother asked, holding the pearls out to her.

Lissa tried to figure out a way to put it diplomatically. In her mind, pearls were for someone older, someone who wore suits or at least elegant dresses. She couldn't imagine wearing them with jeans and a T-shirt. "I don't think I have the right clothes to wear them with," she finally said.

"You're right," her mother said, reluctantly handing the strand back to the saleswoman. "How about a ring? This is lovely." She had the woman take out a blue topaz ring set with three stones.

Lissa slipped it on, the ring huge on her thin finger. The blue stones looked cold, almost icy. They made her shiver. "I don't think so," she said, quickly pulling it off and giving it back.

The saleswoman was losing patience when, ten minutes later, Lissa and her mother left the store empty-handed.

"There's another jewelry store at the far end," her mother said. "I'm sure we'll find something there."

Lissa wanted to leave, wanted to tell her mother that this just wasn't working, but she knew that her mother was determined to find a present. I'll settle for whatever I see that I sort of like and isn't too expensive, Lissa thought.

Just one door before their destination was a pet shop. Lissa, as always, stopped to look at the puppies in the window. This time there were cocker spaniel puppies, all big brown eyes and floppy ears.

"No, Lissa," her mother said with a shake of her head. "You know your father would not allow us to have a dog."

I thought I could have whatever I wanted, Lissa said to herself. I thought I could have whatever would make me happy.

Almost as if she could read Lissa's thoughts, her mother continued. "You know that a dog is bound to bark and carry on, and that would disturb your father."

Lissa had heard this a hundred times, starting from when she was about five years old and began begging for a puppy. She had read just about every animal book ever written while she was in elementary and junior high school, but her requests for a pet had always met instant denial.

She turned to the window on the other side of the pet store entrance. This one held Persian kittens. Lissa melted at the fluffy white fur punctuated by huge blue eyes. She looked at her mother inquiringly.

"Your father is allergic to cats, Lissa. You know that. We've talked about that before."

Her father's allergies were very convenient. They were the perfect excuse for never considering the kittens she had begged for.

Stubbornly Lissa walked into the pet store. Maybe she could get a goldfish or something. It wouldn't disturb her father by making noise, and she'd never heard of goldfish allergies. Granted, it sure wasn't up there with a dog or cat, but maybe it would be better than nothing.

Happy birthday, Lissa. Have a goldfish.

As Lissa walked into the pet store, a flash of green caught her eye on the counter where the cash register sat. The young man working there laughed as a bird climbed onto his finger, then climbed up his shirt sleeve to his shoulder. Once there, the bird nuzzled against his face, then gently bit his ear.

Lissa watched, amazed. She had always thought of birds as pitiful little caged creatures that did nothing but sit behind bars, chirping occasionally.

"What kind of bird is that?" she asked the young man.

"This?" he asked, reaching up to scratch the little green bird's head. The bird rotated his head to get to the exact right spot, then closed his eyes in ecstasy. "He's a gray-cheeked parrot. I'm afraid we all spoil him. He kind of has the run of the store. Do you know anything about these birds?"

"No," Lissa answered, wanting him to go on.

"Well, they're a small member of the parrot family, and they're famous for being tame and sociable. They love to be with people, and they bond very strongly with their owners. They're very special little birds."

"Why doesn't he fly away?" Lissa asked, watching with a smile as the bird scaled back down the man's sleeve, clambering onto the counter, where he promptly picked up the cap of a pen and dropped it on the floor, leaning over the edge to watch it fall.

"His wings are clipped," the man explained. "Here. Let me show you." He gently grasped the bird's wing, extending it. The bird merely looked at him, not at all offended. "The ends of the first five flight feathers are cut," he explained. "That way, he can still fly short distances, but he can't gain altitude. He has enough flight to break his fall if he were to lose his balance, but he can't fly far enough to hurt himself."

"Does it hurt him to have his wings clipped?"

Lissa asked, dreading the thought of pain having been inflicted on the friendly little animal.

"Not at all," the man answered. "There are no nerve endings in the feathers. Besides, he gains a lot of freedom by not being able to fly. This way he doesn't have to be caged. More importantly, he can't fly into anything and break his neck."

"Can he talk?" Lissa asked.

"These particular birds can be taught to talk," the man said. "They're not as good as some of the bigger parrots, but they can be taught. They're very bright birds."

Lissa watched, intrigued, as the bird paraded down the counter, scaling sales receipt pads and a display of dog toys to get to the other end where a small plastic box sat, lid in place. The bird immediately began to work on the lid, using his beak to get leverage.

"His cookies are in there," the man admitted. "He gets a little piece as a treat. He's nuts about them."

"What is he supposed to eat?" Lissa asked, laughing as the bird succeeded in getting the lid off, scaling to the edge of the box, and reaching down to bite off a piece of cookie.

"They need fresh fruit plus water and seed," the man answered.

"Lissa," her mother said warningly, shaking her head.

"Are they noisy?" Lissa persisted.

"They don't squawk constantly, if that's what you mean. This one will sure let you know if he wants attention and you're not giving it to him, but he doesn't fuss without a reason. Plus, he goes to bed at a regular time. It's really funny to watch. At six-thirty every night, he walks to the back of the store, climbs up on his cage, goes up to the top perch, and goes to sleep. That's it. No matter who's in the store or how much commotion there is, he ignores it."

Lissa hesitantly held out her finger to the bird, who had finished his cookie. The bird promptly climbed up on her hand, cocking his head to study her. He gave a low chirp, then nibbled gently on her finger. She held him up to her shoulder, and he hopped off her finger and promptly nestled under her chin. He made a low, growling sound, almost like he was purring.

That did it for Lissa. "This is what I want for my birthday," she said, turning to her mother. "This is the only thing I want. I want this bird."

"Lissa," her mother said despairingly. "You know your father wouldn't want a bird."

A fierce resentment that she had never felt before in her life welled up inside of her. Why did her father always have to get his way? Just once couldn't she get her way? What harm would it do her father for her to have this small green bird? He'd be asleep before her father even came in at night.

"I'll keep him in my room. He won't even know the bird's around."

"Lissa, let's go look at jewelry. Maybe a new pocketbook or shoes or something?"

"The only thing in the world I want is this bird," she said, amazed at her persistence. Still, the bird was cuddled against her neck as if it belonged with her. She could feel its tiny heart beating.

"Lissa, please be reasonable," her mother said.

That did it. Something was snapping inside of her. "Was my father reasonable when he did this?" Lissa said softly, looking down at the cast on her leg. "Was he thinking about my happiness when he did this?" She shoved up the sleeve of her shirt where the fingerprint bruises were still vivid.

Her mother turned pale, looking at the salesman to see if he was listening. Lissa didn't care. She knew that this wasn't fully fair to her mother, but she didn't care about that, either. Where was she when her father was dragging Lissa down the stairs? She was her mother. Shouldn't she help protect her?

She met Lissa's eyes, and Lissa didn't give any ground. She held her gaze until her mother was the one to look away.

"How much does the bird cost?" she asked the man.

"I'm afraid that he's rather expensive since he is a parrot," he said. "He's the only one we have."

"This is the one I want anyway," Lissa said. "This one." She didn't want any gray-cheeked parrot. She wanted *this* gray-cheeked parrot, this sassy little spirit now nuzzled sweetly against her.

Lissa crutched across the store, talking softly to the bird while her mother and the salesman discussed the cost of the bird, cage, and supplies.

"There's one thing you should know," Lissa's mother said, coming over to her as the salesman gathered together the rest. "We can bring this bird back if there are any problems."

Lissa knew exactly what problem she had in mind. She didn't even want to think about it. She gave her mother no response, instead reaching up tentatively to scratch the bird's head.

"Just so you understand," her mother said.

"Thank you for my birthday present," Lissa said, her voice soft and serious.

"Oh, Lissa," her mother said. "There's so much you don't understand. I want you to be happy. I want to see you smile."

"I love this bird," Lissa said. "Thank you."

The bird perched on her finger as they walked through the mall and out to the car, looking around with bright eyes, not the least bit scared. The salesman had wanted to put him in a box, but Lissa wouldn't let him.

She wouldn't let the salesman cage him or shut him up in a box. He wouldn't like that, she knew.

Lissa and her mother didn't talk as they went home. Lissa was studying the small green bird, and her mother was lost in thought, thoughts that undoubtedly involved Lissa's father.

Chapter 12

"Malcolm? Sydney? Reginald?" The next morning at breakfast with her mother, Lissa had auditioned names for the bird who was contentedly eating a piece of apple, perched on her hand.

"Lissa, I think you'd better wait a while before you get too attached to that bird," her mother had answered.

There it was. The threat that hung over her had returned: her father's disapproval. Still, the bird had made it through last night and this morning without being discovered. When she had gotten home the day before, Lissa had spent hours setting up the cage, finding the right spot in her bedroom for it, and acquainting the bird with his new surroundings. The bird had ridden on her shoulder around the yard, explored the house, and walked around her bedroom, eyes bright and inquisitive. Sure enough, at 6:30, while Lissa sat and watched him, he had scaled to the top perch of his cage, fluffed his wings, balanced on one foot, and gone to sleep.

Whenever Lissa had awakened in the night, she had checked for the silhouette of the small green bird in the moonlight that gently lightened her bedroom. The little shape had never moved. Once she got up in the morning, though, the bird had immediately come to life, letting out a loud squawk that brought her running to the cage. She didn't want her father to hear him, even though she knew that he was probably already out in the barn painting. The bird had immediately quieted down once he was on Lissa's shoulder, and now, with a piece of apple, he seemed contented.

Lissa couldn't stand the thought of returning the bird to the pet store. This was her pet, the only one she had ever had, and she was ready to risk even her father's anger to keep him.

Her mother must have sensed the determination that invaded Lissa as she watched the bird eat, pausing every now and then to wipe his beak on the back of her hand. She shifted her leg in its bulky cast into a more comfortable position, and shook her head. No. This bird was hers.

"Please try to understand," her mother said.

"Understand what?" Lissa said. "What is it that you want me to understand?"

"Your father has not had an easy life. It took me a long time to find out about his past. He doesn't like to talk about it."

"What could make him refuse to let me have this bird? Is that too much to ask for?" Lissa's voice was quiet but forceful. "I have never asked him for much, have I?"

"No, Lissa, it's not that. It's not that at all."

"Then explain it to me," Lissa said. "Help me to understand." To herself she thought, there's nothing that will help me to understand taking back this bird. The mere thought of handing him back to the pet store salesman made her panic.

"I don't know how much to tell you," her mother said, turning her back to Lissa and looking out the kitchen window toward the barn. It wasn't as if her father was likely to walk in on them. He never came in during the day.

"He's my father," Lissa said fiercely. "This is my only family. Don't I deserve to know?"

"I suppose you do," her mother said after a quiet moment's reflection. "I suppose I should have told you some of this before."

Lissa waited. It seemed to take forever before her mother began to speak again.

"Your father's parents were not educated or sophisticated people. Your grandfather worked in the coal mines in western Pennsylvania — hard, backbreaking, dangerous work — and your grandmother worked in the grocery store in the small town where they lived. They were honest, hardworking people who never finished high school or thought much beyond surviving day to day. They didn't quite know what to make of someone like your father."

"Was he their only child?" Lissa asked.

"Yes. His mother had a terrible time giving birth to him, and she could never have any more children. I guess that really disappointed his father, who had planned to have a big family."

"So he was an only child like me," Lissa said, thinking that perhaps that was one way that she and her father were alike.

"Yes, but I don't think it was a very happy family," her mother continued.

Like this one? Lissa thought, but instead of hurting her mother, she merely scratched the bird's head and listened.

"Your father's parents, especially his father, never accepted the idea that he loved to draw and wanted to be an artist. In fact, your father used to get beaten whenever his father saw him drawing. He said it was a waste of time that could be better spent accomplishing something, doing work, earning money to help the family. He made your father work for the local farmers after school and in the summers from the time he was ten years old."

"But my father kept drawing?" Lissa asked.

"Yes," her mother continued. "He said that it was like it was beyond his control. He had to. Even though he had to hide his pictures, he always found a way to draw."

Perhaps Lissa and her father had more in common than she thought, even though Lissa knew that she had no talent.

"It got much worse as he got older," her mother said after another pause to gather her thoughts. "His father found some of his drawings and accused his son of being gay."

"He said that to my father?" Lissa asked.

"All the time," her mother answered. "He just couldn't understand someone who was so different from himself. He had envisioned his son as following in his footsteps, and your father wasn't willing to do that."

"What about his mother?" Lissa asked.

"She worked long hours so your father was left to his own devices a lot. He doesn't talk much about her, but I get the sense that she pretty much agreed with her husband. She wanted him to settle down and get an honest job and marry a local girl and give her grandbabies."

How sad, Lissa thought.

"How did he escape?" Lissa asked.

"He enlisted in the Army," her mother said.

"I didn't know that," Lissa said in amazement. It was hard to imagine her father in the military, dressing like everyone else, following orders, being shoved around by someone else.

"I didn't know until after we were married," her mother admitted. "It is a subject he truly refuses to discuss. All I know is that he had an especially horrible fight with his father right after he graduated from high school. His parents had refused to give him any money toward college, and he wanted to get away from them and out of that town more than anything in the world."

"So he enlisted in the Army?" Lissa asked.

"And promptly got sent to Vietnam," her mother said.

"My father was in Vietnam?" Lissa asked in amazement. He had actually been in the jungles, fighting? She thought back to movies she had seen, and it was impossible to put her father into such a setting.

"He was in the jungles during the last year of the war. He came home a few months before the peace treaty was signed. And that, Lissa, is all I know. That's a part of his life that he has put behind him."

Lissa's mind was filled with a thousand questions. Had he been shot at? Had he killed anybody? Had he had friends killed? Had it been as terrible as it looked in the movies she had seen?

Somehow she doubted that she'd have a chance to find out. After all, she and her father didn't even talk about normal things like school. How was she going to get him to discuss Vietnam?

"What happened next?" Lissa asked.

"He came back, went to college on the G.I. Bill and got a degree in art, painted every free second, and eventually ended up teaching in the college where I met him. You know the rest."

"What about his parents?"

Again, Lissa's mother hesitated, but finally she turned to face her daughter and answered her. "His mother died of cancer while he was in the Army."

"And his father?"

"He's still alive," her mother said after a long pause.

"He's alive? I have a grandfather?"

"Yes, but your father hasn't seen him or spoken to him since the day he left for the Army."

"So he doesn't even know about you? He doesn't know that I exist?"

"I doubt it," her mother said. "Your father never wanted him to know anything about his life."

"Don't you think he'd be happy to know that his son is now a successful artist?"

"It's a subject I've learned not to bring up with your father. He won't even consider getting in contact with him. He says he wouldn't recognize his father if he passed him on the street, and that's the way he wants it."

"How sad," Lissa said.

"I know, but that's the way your father wants it."

So that's the way it will be, Lissa thought.

Her mind raced, trying to absorb this new knowledge. She had known that her mother's parents had died within a year of each other when her mother was in her early twenties, so Lissa had never known them. Because she had never heard her father's parents mentioned, she had assumed that they were dead, too.

She had a grandfather. She had dreamed of

having grandparents when she was a little girl, grandparents who would spoil her rotten and give her presents, grandparents she would go to visit during summer vacation.

Now she knew that she had a grandfather who didn't know she existed, and probably didn't care.

So much for all of those nice stories in the books she read.

Lissa's mother lapsed into silence, and soon afterward, seemed agitated and restless. She left saying that she had errands to run. Balancing carefully on her crutches, the bird perched on her shoulder, Lissa went out into the yard and settled under a tree, letting the bird explore in the lower branches, keeping a careful eye on him to be certain that he did not venture out of her reach.

Perhaps now she could better understand her father's anger. What, though, was her role in this? Because his father had not loved him, he would not love Lissa? Or was it that she was a disappointment to him, just as he had been to his father?

What part of the family history was being lived out again by Lissa and her father?

She thought and thought, trying to find the answers, as the small green bird played in the tree above her.

Chapter 13

The rest of that summer, leading up to the day that Lissa's world as she knew it had ended, passed in a relaxed haze. She had spent countless hours playing with Bird. That, unfortunately, was what he had ended up being named. By the time Lissa felt confident that her father would continue to ignore the bird just as he ignored her, she had delayed giving him a name and called him "bird" for so long that it became his name. Trying to give him another simply hadn't worked.

She had taught him to talk. Thousands of repetitions of "Pretty Bird" convinced him to say it. Within weeks, however, he had elaborated. He began saying, "Pretty pretty bird bird bird," which even Lissa had to admit was an improvement over the first version. Eventually he also learned to say "What are you doing?" although for some reason he refused to say "Hello." He was a spirited, ornery, strong-willed creature, and he completely stole Lissa's heart. When she lay down on her bed to read, he lay on her stomach or against her neck, more like a cat than a bird. When Lissa got her cast off and began to walk further and further each day to strengthen her leg, Bird was her constant companion, riding on her shoulder or on top of her head. She learned his vocabulary of noises: the "ratchety-ratchety" holler that he used only for people he knew, the screech of anger when he wanted attention, the clicking sound that meant that he was contented.

June slid through to July and August. Lissa had books and Bird, enough to while away the summer days, plus daydreams of finishing her senior year and going away to college. Her only concern was that she find a place that would allow Bird to accompany her. Still, she was convinced she would find a way. If she couldn't keep him in a dorm room, she'd simply have to get a room off-campus. Bird was not negotiable. He was now a part of her.

Lissa knew that most people would think she was crazy for caring so much about a little green bird. It was okay to care about a dog or a cat, but a bird? Even her mother shook her head in amazement at the bond between Lissa and Bird. She figured that her father must be aware of the animal's existence in the house, but she did her best to keep him out of sight, and her father had become almost invisible. He rose before dawn to go to the barn, totally absorbed in a new work that her mother said would be his masterpiece. It was often midnight or after when he came into the house. Her mother made fleeting visits to take him food, but otherwise he might have lived in another town.

As long as that meant Lissa could keep Bird, she figured it was a fair trade.

Only two other people knew about Bird, and they were a part of her new life. Josh was one. Josh's grandmother was the other. Once again Lissa found herself traveling to thoughts of Josh. She couldn't help jumping forward in thought.

Lissa remembered how it had started.

"Lissa, I have a huge favor to ask of you. I know that you're not going to want to do it, but I want you to hear me out before you say no. It's not as bad an idea as you think, and it will make a really nice person very, very happy, and I know you'd like to do that, wouldn't you?" Josh's words bombarded Lissa the second that she got to her seat in English class.

Even she had to smile. His boundless enthusiasm was more that of a child than a high school student, but it was refreshing compared to all of the guys who acted tough and mean and made crude comments. "What?" she asked.

"My grandmother's birthday is next week, and I need a very special present for her," Josh said. With that the bell rang to begin class. "Meet me at the side door next to the tennis courts at lunch and I'll explain," he said quickly. "Please, Lissa?"

She had nodded, then spent the rest of the morning wondering why she had agreed. Still, she walked toward the exit at lunch, half expecting that he wouldn't be there. He was, and his face lit up in a huge smile when he saw her.

"I figured the odds were about fifty to one that you wouldn't come. Thank you, Lissa," he said. "Here. It's a bribe." He led her outside to a bench near the tennis courts, then held out a crumpled brown bag to her. "It had a rough morning in my bookbag. Sorry."

Lissa opened the bag and took out a piece of cake wrapped in plastic. The top was golden brown, the middle filled with cinnamon and apples.

"It's my specialty — apple cake," Josh said proudly.

"You baked this?" Lissa asked, opening it and breaking off a bite. "It's delicious."

"Your amazement is sexist," Josh said, his voice filled with indignation. "Just because I'm a male, you think I can't bake? My grandmother made sure that I could bake and cook from the time I was knee-high to a grasshopper. That's one of her expressions, in case you couldn't tell."

Lissa had to smile. She couldn't help it.

"My grandmother is the reason I'm bribing you," Josh said. "You have to understand that I absolutely adore her. I've spent half my life at her house. If my parents would have let me, I'd have lived with her. It's like we're kindred spirits. She's going to be seventy, but you'd swear she's about forty. She picks strawberries, makes homemade pickles, watches MTV, and bakes the best bread on the face of the earth." Josh's face was alive with joy as he talked about his grandmother.

"I want to get her something really special, and I've searched and searched, and I can't find the right thing."

"Bake her one of these," Lissa said, breaking off another bite of the moist, delicious cake.

"Of course I'll bake her a birthday cake. That goes without saying," Josh said. "Still, I need the perfect present, and I've figured out what it is. The only thing is, you have to help me."

"Me? What can I do?" Lissa asked.

"My grandmother loves animals," Josh said. "I swear that she can talk to them, and they talk back. I've never seen anything like it."

"Does she like birds?" Lissa asked.

"She has a catbird that waits out in her yard for her each day, and they whistle back and forth, carry on whole conversations," Josh said with a laugh. "That bird sits in the tree outside her kitchen window and waits for her. I've seen it with my own eyes. I wouldn't lie to you."

"I have a bird," Lissa said, the words out before she could stop them.

"You do? What kind? That's great!"

Haltingly, Lissa told him a little about Bird, his breed, size, personality, warming to the telling as she went. She was amazed to find that she had gone on about Bird for almost five minutes before she suddenly halted. She never talked this much to people. Still, Josh was different.

"My grandmother would love you," Josh said. "I bet she'd love to meet Bird."

That can't happen, Lissa automatically thought. I've already said too much.

"Anyway," Josh said, "here's the request. I want you to draw one of your pictures with all the little creatures for my grandmother. I'll get it matted and framed, and it will be the best birthday present I've ever given her. She would love it, Lissa. I know she would. Please say yes. I'll pay you. I'll bake a whole cake just for you. I'll be your devoted servant for the next fourteen years. What do you say?"

Lissa's heart sank. She couldn't do that. "I'm sorry," she said. "I never let anyone have my drawings. They're not good enough."

"Lissa, the one I saw was wonderful. Besides, all that matters is that my grandmother would love it. Please say yes."

"I can't," Lissa said. The thought of her work out where people could see it and mock it made her stomach ache.

"I don't see why not," Josh said stubbornly. "It wouldn't kill you to do this."

That's what you think, Lissa thought, wishing she could explain, knowing that she couldn't.

Chapter 14

What was it about Josh? Although Lissa had stubbornly resisted his pleas to draw a picture for his grandmother, that evening she spent hours and hours sketching. Time after time she threw away the results, each not meeting her critical standards. She was amazed to look up at her clock and discover that it was one in the morning. Great, she thought. School tomorrow, and she'd have, at most, five hours of sleep. Still, she had not torn up the last picture lying on her desk. It was the most detailed that she had ever drawn, tiny, finely worked, with spirits and creatures hidden in every nook.

It wasn't good enough; she knew that. She could hear her father's ridicule: trite, childish, poorly done. She would tear it up in the morning.

But she hadn't. Instead, she had carefully placed it inside her English book and taken it to school with her. That didn't mean she had to show it to Josh, she reassured herself.

But she did. She would never know what impulse had caused her to place the picture on his desk. Although she insisted that it wasn't worthy to be shown to anybody, deep down she had to admit that she was pleased by his praise.

"Lissa, it's wonderful. My grandmother will love it. What can I pay you or give you or do for you in exchange?"

Lissa had only meant to show it to him. She hadn't meant to let him keep it. His enthusiasm, though, was boundless. What harm would it do? Surely his grandmother would just shove it in a drawer somewhere. It wasn't good enough to display.

"Sign it, Lissa," Josh had insisted.

"No," Lissa had answered quickly. "No."

"Why not? You should be proud of this. If I could draw something this good, I'd tell the world it was mine."

"No," Lissa repeated. "I can't sign it. I won't."

Josh must have seen her determination because he backed off.

"Will you at least come meet my grandmother? I know she'll be dying to meet you after she sees this."

"I go home right after school," Lissa said.

"I'd be glad to run you home. I think you'd really like my grandmother, especially since you both like birds so much."

"I'm sure I would," Lissa said, committing to nothing, relieved when the bell rang for class. What was she thinking? Why was she even thinking about Josh and his grandmother? That wasn't what she wanted. It wasn't part of the deal. It wasn't safe.

The next day Josh was waiting for Lissa when her bus arrived at school. By Josh standards, he was quiet, almost subdued. "Thank you very much," he said, holding out his hand which had been tucked behind his back.

Lissa took the single red rose. "You didn't have to."

"I know. I wanted to." Josh looked at Lissa as they walked toward the front door of the school, shaking his head. "Why do you make it so hard?" he finally asked.

"What do you mean?" Lissa asked, getting nervous.

"Is it that you just don't like me?" Josh asked. "I mean, I'm always paying attention to you, trying to get you to do things with me, and you're always making excuses. If you just hate me, tell me and I'll leave you alone."

"I don't hate you," Lissa said. The words were out before she could stop herself. After all, he had given her the perfect opportunity to shut him out completely. Still, she couldn't say those words. Not to him.

"Well, that's a relief. How about we run away and get married and have fourteen kids?"

"What?" Lissa asked, astonishment ringing in her voice.

"Okay, if you won't do that, why don't you go to the movies with me this weekend?"

Before Lissa could begin making excuses, Josh cut her off. "Just think about it, okay?" Before she could say anything, he gave her a grin and dashed off.

Great, Lissa thought. Now she'd have to wait until English to tell him no.

She walked slowly down the hallway toward her homeroom, each step filling her heart with more bitterness.

Why couldn't she live a normal life?

Why did she have to shut out everybody?

Why couldn't she do a simple thing like go to the movies with a guy on a Saturday night? Was that too much to ask?

Of course it was.

After all, there was nothing normal about her life anymore.

Not since that day.

Not since the day that her father almost killed her.

Chapter 15

Let this be over, Lissa thought, listening for the footsteps. She had not heard them for a while, but she did not even consider the possibility that they would not return, that she was safe.

She was not safe.

She would never again believe that she could be safe.

She had hoped that moving here was the answer, but it hadn't been. That was obvious. If it had been the answer, would she be cowering at the base of a tree, hidden by leaves, thinking back over her life as she prepared to die?

Silly Lissa. Imagine even thinking that she could fight back, that she could win.

Besides, Bird would get restless any minute, and his fussing would draw attention. She couldn't blame him. After all, he was hungry and cold and confused.

Like her.

As Lissa felt her mind drift away, she yanked it back. It would be so easy, she thought, to just let go, but she hadn't remembered this much not to face the final memory. She was losing hope of understanding. The clarity, the answers she had hoped to discover weren't coming to her. Instead, she just felt sad.

Sad that she would never again see Josh's smile. She had never told him how much his smiles had meant to her. She hadn't even admitted it to herself. Now she would never have a chance. Josh, she thought, thank you. You have been the only beacon of light in the darkness that has become my life.

Except for Bird, that is. Thank you, she said silently to the little green bird beginning to stir under her hand. You have made me laugh. You have taught me that size doesn't matter as much as spirit. You have more determination than creatures a hundred times your size, and you prove what is important: security, warmth, determination, affection. All you ask is that I feed you and provide you with a safe place to sleep and give you attention and let you explore your world.

Was that too much to ask? It wasn't for a small green bird. It had been too much for Lissa to ask for, though.

It was time. It was time to think back on the day, the one that had led inevitably to this day.

What could she have done differently? What could she have done to prevent all of this? How much of it was her fault?

She and Bird had been walking across the yard toward the tree where a low branch was Bird's favorite place to play. He would prance up and down the limb, pecking at the bark and keeping a constant eye on Lissa, making sure that she didn't stray too far away. If she did, his screams of protest would bring her back, holding out her finger for Bird, who would come to her and then climb to her shoulder, tucking in against her neck, clucking softly to remind her that he wasn't to be left too far behind.

They were almost to the tree, Bird already perched on her finger, ready to be lifted up to the branch, when the door of the barn crashed back on its hinges. Lissa froze. It was only ten o'clock in the morning. What was her father doing out? She had never even considered the possibility that he would cross the yard; if she had, she and Bird would have stayed in her room.

Her father had a distracted look on his face as he walked quickly across the yard, running his hands through his hair, shoulder-length and shaggy. He had on jeans and a black T-shirt, hands and shirt stained with vivid orange and red and green paint.

Maybe he won't see us, Lissa thought. She didn't move. Bird, however, was watching her father intently. He leaned toward his direction, and hollered the call he used for people who were familiar to him, that "ratchety-ratchety" sound. Lissa was surprised to hear Bird use that call for her father, since the two had not even really met.

Lissa's father stopped abruptly. It was as if he were a movie that suddenly went to freeze frame. He was about twenty yards away from Lissa, but she could feel his eyes lock onto her. She gave up hoping that he wouldn't notice her, but she still figured that he would go on his way. He had not spoken to her in months, not since the night that her leg got broken.

"Ratchety-ratchety," Bird called again, bobbing his head in greeting. "Ratchety-ratchety."

The sound seemed to transform her father. He covered the twenty yards between them so quickly that it was almost magical, gliding more than running. As he got to within feet of her, Lissa held out her hand, showing him Bird. Her mind raced. No matter what, he can't make me get rid of Bird, she thought desperately. He's mine.

"This is my bird," she said as he got to her. "He's no trouble at all."

Before she could continue, her father snatched Bird off of her finger. She heard Bird's startled cry as her father's fist closed around him.

No. He would not hurt Bird. She wouldn't let him. "Give him to me," she screamed, lunging for his hand. "Don't you dare hurt him."

She expected her father to scream back. She had never, not once in her entire life, yelled at her father. She expected a huge reaction but there was none. His eyes were cold and distant, almost vacant. He didn't say a word in response. Instead, he flung Bird away from him. Lissa watched in horror as the tiny bundle of iridescent green feathers thudded to the ground.

"Bird," she cried, frantic to get to him.

Then she felt the arm around her neck. Without her even being aware of his movement, he had crossed behind her, whipping his arm around her neck so that his forearm crushed against her throat. She clawed desperately, trying to break his grip, trying to see if Bird was moving, trying to fight through the complete and utter confusion that was washing over her mind.

Then she heard her father's voice, a harsh whisper against her ear. "You're already dead."

For a moment, he released the pressure of his arm, and Lissa gasped desperately for air, trying at the same time to duck under his arm and get away. Why is he doing this, she thought desperately. He can be angry because I have an animal that he didn't know about, but why this?

She didn't have long to think. The release of his arm had only been a momentary respite. She felt his hands, fingers powerful, close around her throat.

"You're already dead," came the voice again, cold and distant. Lissa struggled futilely, feeling the dizziness, the pain, the coming darkness. Bird, she thought. Bird.

She didn't know how much later it was when she regained consciousness. She was aware of the pain, the throbbing of her head, the tightness in her throat that made each breath a struggle. She was on the ground, one arm outstretched. She opened her eyes, amazed to see sunlight. How could there be light when all had been darkness?

Then, moving through grass that was almost as high as he was, came Bird. He was silent, finding his way hesitantly, giving a small cry when he got to her outstretched hand and nuzzled under it.

Bird, she tried to say, but she couldn't get any words out of her damaged throat. Bird. She closed her hand gently around him and pulled him close, curling her body over his, sheltering him.

Then the tears came, streaming unbidden, unnoticed down her face.

She didn't know how much later it was that her mother came rushing out into the yard, frantically asking what was wrong, had she fallen, was it her leg?

Lissa, tucked into a fetal position on the ground, refused to answer. Her mother eventually knelt beside her and forced her head up. She gave a low moan when Lissa's neck was revealed.

"Who did this, Lissa?"

Lissa looked at her dully.

"Lissa, who did this to you? What happened?"

"My father did this." Lissa forced out the words through the pain. "My father tried to kill me."

"No," Lissa's mother said.

Lissa stared at her. No? Why would she doubt her own daughter? No?

Lissa curled back up, tucking herself into the shelter of the ground, cradling the body of the small green bird.

Chapter 16

Lissa's mother had watched in horror as her husband came crashing back out of the house and took off on foot down the driveway that led to the road. He never left at this time of day, rarely ever left at all. She stared at Lissa, stunned, tears streaking her face. "Your father did this?" she asked, touching Lissa's throat.

"He said I was already dead, and he tried to strangle me," Lissa said, suddenly strangely calm. The words could hardly be heard through the increasing pressure of her swollen, sore throat.

"Maybe he was just upset, angry about his work."

Lissa couldn't figure out what she felt: anger? betrayal? resignation? She had just told her mother, the person who loved her best on the face of the earth, that someone had tried to kill her, and her mother was making excuses for him? What hope was there? Suddenly, though, anger won. She had not asked to be born, to be fathered by that man, to be placed into these lives. Those choices were not hers; how high was the price she was supposed to pay?

She struggled to sit up, being mindful to keep Bird cradled carefully in her hand. She was reassured by the constant, rapid heartbeat that she felt. At least her father hadn't killed him.

"I will not live here," she said, meeting the eyes of her mother who was sitting on the ground beside her. "He is going to kill me. I'm not safe here."

"Lissa, I'll be more careful. I'll keep a better watch over you. I won't let him be alone with you."

"That's not good enough," Lissa said, wondering where this strength was coming from. "You didn't protect me today, and you can't always be there."

"Yes I can, Lissa. Now that I know how bad things are, how explosive he is, I'll be much more careful."

"I can't live like that," Lissa said. "Either you find me another place to live, or I'm going to go to the police or Child Protective Services or my school counselor or someone. I'll tell the world that my father, the famous artist, tried to kill me."

"Lissa," her mother moaned.

"I'm not going to let him kill Bird, and I'm not going to let him kill me," Lissa said, then sank back so that her aching head rested on the ground again. Her throat hurt so badly that it was a struggle to swallow, and her hands suddenly began to shake. My father tried to kill me, she thought, almost unable to comprehend the thought. I can't live here, and my mother doesn't really believe me or understand.

"I'm sorry, Lissa," her mother said, stroking her daughter's hair. "I don't know what is going on that is making your father behave like this, but it can't go on. I couldn't bear for something to happen to you."

Something already has happened, Lissa thought. First my leg, and now this.

"I just don't know where to go," she said. "I don't have any family, and I haven't kept in touch with any of my old friends."

Maybe it was as simple as that. Her father wanted her mother completely focused on him and his life, and he had isolated her from the rest of the world with his demands and his lifestyle. Now he wanted to isolate her from Lissa, too.

"My grandfather?" Lissa whispered.

"Oh, Lissa, I don't think we can count on him. He doesn't even know we exist, and he and your father had a terrible relationship anyway. I don't think he'd welcome you with open arms."

I'm going to have to stay here, Lissa thought. I'm going to have to die.

"But that doesn't matter," Lissa's mother said. "Can you walk? We need to get you out of here."

Lissa got to her feet, her head spinning. She walked slowly to the house and up to her bedroom, tears streaming down her face as she looked at the canopy bed, the rows of books that had been her refuge. Still, there was no longer any refuge, any safety in this house. Her father had taken care of that.

She discovered that once she accepted that she could not take all of her books, she cared about very little. She packed clothes, notebooks, and Bird's supplies. She realized that she had no photographs, no mementos from family trips or vacations, no gifts from friends.

Her mother had packed equally simply, and they loaded suitcases into the trunk and Bird's cage into the back seat of the car. Lissa took a towel to put on her lap and kept Bird with her. He seemed unnerved but healthy, willing to eat some apple and drink a sip of water before she got into the car with him.

They drove. Lissa's mother admitted that she had no specific destination in mind, but they simply headed west and drove. With each passing mile, Lissa felt a tiny bit of the tension leave her. He wouldn't follow. He wouldn't find her. She would be safe.

After four hours, Lissa's mother pulled into a motel, leaving Lissa in the car until she had paid for a room with cash, and then parked the car right in front of the door to the room. She said it was so that the manager wouldn't see Bird, but Lissa suspected that it was also so that nobody would see the vivid purple bruises that ringed her neck.

As soon as Lissa got Bird settled, she lay down on the bed. She refused her mother's offer to go get food for her, accepting only some aspirin and a soda from the machine outside. She lay in silence, trying to shut off her mind and the questions that tortured her. Eventually she slept.

The next day, Lissa's mother had seemed energized. By nine o'clock, she had driven to the nearest town, a small place that actually had a Main Street, and was parked in front of a realtor's office. Leaving Lissa and Bird in the car, she was only inside for about twenty minutes before coming back out, a smiling young woman right behind her. Lissa heard her mother insist that she'd follow in her own car.

The house that the realtor took them to was miles outside of town, down a series of smaller and smaller and smaller roads. Years before it had been the caretaker's house for a large hunting lodge used a few weeks a year by a millionaire who lived the rest of the year in Hawaii. The lodge had burned down, the millionaire had died, and his estate had been tied up for years in court. His heirs, however, had rented out the caretaker's house, the last renters having left only a week before.

Lissa, her neck covered by a high turtleneck, drew confused looks from the realtor since the temperature was in the high eighties, but Lissa's silence did not seem to bother her. The lady rattled on to her mother about the birds and wildlife that lived in the surrounding woods, the tranquility of the setting, the fact that it had total privacy yet was only about ten miles from town. The perfect little getaway, she called it.

If only she knew what Lissa was getting away from.

Lissa's mother had rented the house as soon as Lissa agreed that she felt safe there. It was ironic, Lissa thought. Normally she would be apprehensive about the isolation, the wild animals, the fact that no other houses were visible. Now, though, the isolation made her feel better, as long as it isolated her from the one person who mattered.

The house was fully furnished. The furniture was worn but comfortable, and the kitchen had all of the essentials. Lissa's mother left her to explore while she went to buy towels and food. Lissa chose her bedroom, the smaller of the two but the one with the best view. The two windows both looked out on the back woods, and outside one window a huge holly tree rose up, its branches brushing the house. She placed Bird's cage where he could look out into the woods, and he rode on her shoulder as she unpacked.

After her mother got back, they walked around the house. The driveway that led to the house wound through a stretch of trees, but there was no dense underbrush, just scattered bushes and weeds. The sides and back were not exactly yard, but the remnants of grassy areas still remained. The woods started out relatively tamely, but within two hundred yards the underbrush became thick and tangled. Bird seemed excited by his new surroundings. Lissa found a low branch for him to perch on, and he pranced up and down, occasionally hanging upside down by one foot, calling out for Lissa if she strayed more than a few feet away from him.

That afternoon, Lissa and her mother, without Bird this time, went to the office of the local school district and registered Lissa for her senior year. Lissa had asked about the possibility of using a different last name, but her mother said that they wouldn't have enough documentation to be able to do that. Besides, they would need to send for her transcripts from her old school. Lissa tried to put away her fears. After all, she was hours away in a remote little town, and her father wouldn't even want to find her. Besides, their last name, Davis, was a common one. Nobody would associate her with her father. She would attract no attention. She would make sure of that.

For a few days, Lissa and her mother kept busy setting up their new house. Her mother made numerous trips to town on errands, and Lissa learned to listen to the woods, to hear the birds and the rustling of the squirrels and rabbits as friendly sounds, not threatening ones. The pain in her throat began to ease, and the purple of the bruises began to turn yellow.

It took a couple of days before her mother became restless, unable to sit still or focus on any task. Lissa waited, knowing what was coming.

"Lissa," her mother finally said, pacing back and forth in the living room as her daughter read in the chair by the window. "I need to know what is going on with your father. I have to find out if he's home."

Lissa had no doubt that her mother had tried to call him every time she went out; it was only today that their own phone had been hooked up.

"I don't want you to feel that I am abandoning you, or that I approve of what he did to you," her mother said in a rush.

But you still love him, Lissa thought, studying the torment in her mother's face. If you didn't, you'd never want to see him again. There wouldn't be any torment.

"Just promise me that you won't tell him anything, anything at all, about where I am," Lissa said fiercely, knowing that she couldn't keep her mother away. "He can't know where I am."

"I know that, Lissa. I won't do anything to put you in any danger. I just have to see if he . . ."

"If he's okay," Lissa finished for her.

"Yes," her mother said. "Please don't hate me."

"I know that you love him," Lissa said. "I know that you've built your whole life around him."

"And around you," her mother said.

"And me," Lissa said softly.

"I'll be back by dark," her mother said, racing to collect her keys and her pocketbook, wanting out before Lissa made it difficult.

"Don't worry. I'll be fine here," Lissa said. "Just don't say anything that will even give him a clue."

"I love you, Lissa," her mother said, hugging her fiercely. Then she was gone.

Lissa was unable to settle back down to her book so she put Bird on her shoulder and went for a walk into the edge of the woods. She couldn't say that she was surprised by her mother's departure. It was hard to understand that her mother still cared about the man who had tried to kill her daughter, but then, what about this made sense?

Besides, Lissa thought, let's be practical. One more year of high school and then she was off to college and her own life. Then her mother and father could have their own intense, private little life. He could play the temperamental artistic genius, and her mother could be the invisible force behind him.

Still, this would work. Lissa would live in the little house in the woods while she finished her senior year. She'd keep a low profile, attract no attention to herself. That wouldn't be hard. Then she'd go far away to college. More and more she thought that she would have to live in a little apartment off campus. She couldn't imagine living in a dormitory full of laughing girls who worried about things like hair and homecoming and friends. What would she have in common with them?

Besides, she didn't want to have to be asked why she never went home over holidays or summer vacation. How could she explain that she could never go home again?

Yes, she and Bird would live in their own little place far away. Her mother could come and visit once in a while.

All she had to do was get through her invisible senior year.

Chapter 17

The school year began and Lissa found her new school not that much different from her old one. Except, of course, this one included Josh. Lissa and her mother settled into a routine of sorts. The bus picked Lissa up about a half mile down the back road, and Lissa discovered that she enjoyed the walk. In the morning she took the time to think through her schedule, running through her classes, reassuring herself that she was ready for each of them. In the afternoon she thought back over the day and planned what she needed to do that evening.

She knew, even though they did not discuss it, that many days, if not most, her mother drove the four hours home to see Lissa's father, coming back to Lissa by early evening. That first time she had left, Lissa had been waiting anxiously for her return.

Lissa's mother looked haggard and tired, the lines at her forehead and mouth much more pronounced than usual. She looked at Lissa nervously, and Lissa let the silence drag. Finally, she gave in.

"Was he there?" she asked.

"Yes," her mother answered.

"Did he say why he did it?" Lissa asked. Her nightmares had been filled with that confusion.

"He's not talking much," her mother said.

That's great, Lissa thought. That's not a bad life if you can manage it. You almost kill somebody, but hey, if you don't want to talk about it, you can just ignore it. It will go away.

No, she thought, I will go away.

For a moment, she wondered if her father had even noticed that she was gone.

Her mother must have read the mixture of anger and disgust that Lissa was feeling. She didn't say anything more about her trip home.

That, too, became a pattern. When she came home in the evening, they acted like her mother was coming home from a long day at the office. Lissa guessed, in a weird way, that her father was her mother's job.

One morning Lissa's bus had been very late, and her mother had driven past her while she waited at the bus stop. She remembered the guilty look on her mother's face, as if she were a rebellious teenager sneaking out the window past curfew to meet the guy her parents had forbidden her to see.

And Lissa had put into action her plan for an invisible senior year. She got all A's, part of her plan for getting accepted at colleges far away, and she got involved in no activities, made no friends. Once the girls realized that she was no threat to them, they ignored her. Once the guys realized that she was smart and that she wouldn't flirt with them, they ignored her, too.

Except Josh.

And that was one big exception.

Lissa was dismayed to find out how often her thoughts strayed to Josh. At night when she was studying, his smile would flash through her mind, driving away calculus equations and verb conjugations.

No, Lissa told herself firmly. Josh was a risk she could not take. Anybody was a risk she couldn't take. After all, look what could happen. The first thing she knew, Josh would be asking questions. Tell me about your family. What does your father do? Where did you live before you moved here? Those were normal, everyday questions that people expected to have answered.

Except Lissa couldn't answer them.

She knew that. It was just that Josh was so persistent, and so sweet in his persistence. After she gave him the drawing for his grandmother, he refused to accept that she wouldn't go out with him. Just a movie, he insisted. Nothing fancy, nothing extravagant. Just a way to thank her for what she had done.

No, Lissa said. The worst part was that she couldn't tell him why. She could see the hurt in his eyes, and she couldn't tell him that it wasn't personal. There was nothing she would rather do than something simple and normal like go out on a date with a boy who was being nice to her.

A boy she liked a great deal, she had to admit to herself. She found herself looking forward to English, to his silly comments.

"I've sulked for the last twenty-four hours since you refused to go out with me," he announced one day, "but I'm over it now."

"Good," Lissa said gently.

"But I'm not giving up," he said firmly. "You think that you can reject me and reject me, and eventually I'll just shrivel up and go away. Well, you haven't met the likes of me before."

"No," Lissa admitted. "I've never known anybody like you before."

"You're my senior year challenge," Josh said

with a spirited grin. "I'm going to get a date with Lissa Davis or die in the process."

Oh Josh, Lissa thought despairingly. Don't even joke about dying.

"Besides, we're practically neighbors," Josh continued.

Lissa stopped breathing. What did he mean? Had he been following her? Nobody knew where she lived. How had he found out?

"What?" she gasped.

"Don't look so surprised," Josh laughed. "This is a small town, remember? My mother's second cousin twice removed is the real estate lady who rented you and your mother the caretaker's cottage at the old lodge."

Lissa didn't know whether to be relieved or upset. At least he had gained the information innocently enough.

Still, if he knew where she lived, then others could find out. Stop this, she lectured herself. How likely was it that her father would track her down? He had what he wanted now. She was gone, and he didn't even have blood on his hands.

The risk of getting close to Josh was still too great, though. What would they talk about? She couldn't talk about her past, her family, anything. She'd just be a mute blob that would bore him to death, anyway.

Josh deserved better than her. He deserved somebody to share with him his unbounded joy in life. He deserved somebody who could tell him stories about when she was younger, stories that did not involve broken legs and nearly broken necks. Sure, she could tell him about Bird, but how long would he want to listen to that? No, Josh was a mistake. She could not afford to make mistakes.

Still, that smile.

Her mind was drifting to Josh that day in English class when the message arrived.

"Lissa. Lissa!" Her teacher's amused voice roused her from her reverie. Josh was tapping her shoulder frantically.

"Yes?" Lissa said, face flushing. Had the teacher called on her while she was daydreaming? What was the question?

"This message is for you." The teacher held out a slip of paper, and an envelope. Lissa vaguely remembered now that a knock on the door had interrupted class.

Lissa walked to the front of the room to take the message. The slip of paper merely had her name, the name of her teacher, and the room number. The envelope was white, legal-sized, unstamped, with no return address. Her name was on it, written in neat block letters. Written at the bottom were the words: Please deliver to above student immediately.

Lissa returned to her seat, studying the envelope intently. What was it? Maybe it was from her counselor. She'd met with him repeatedly to discuss options for college. Still, wouldn't he just call her down to his office?

Suddenly she thought of an explanation. It must be from her mother. Maybe she was going to be later than usual and didn't want Lissa to worry. Lissa knew that her mother had left for home before Lissa had even left for school, muttering something about a meeting. She had figured that her father was meeting with a gallery owner or something and wanted her mother along. Maybe her plans had changed. Maybe she was spending the night.

Lissa ripped open the envelope impatiently. Why hadn't her mother simply called her later? Still, dropping by the school was only a few blocks out of her way as she left town.

Lissa unfolded the single sheet of paper, heavy and rough, torn at one edge.

Her gasp when she saw the words written on it stopped her English class in its tracks.

Chapter 18

"Lissa, what is it?" her English teacher asked in the silence that followed Lissa's horrified gasp.

"I have to leave," Lissa said, frantically gathering up her books.

"Is it a family emergency?" the teacher asked, face filled with concern.

Lissa hesitated only briefly. "Yes."

"I'm so sorry," the teacher said. "Do you want me to go down to the office with you?"

"I'll go," Josh said.

"No," Lissa said sharply. She did not want him involved in this.

"That's a good idea," the teacher said. "Thank you, Josh."

Lissa dashed out the door, not wanting to linger to argue. She'd get away from Josh once she was out of the classroom.

"Lissa, what's wrong? You look like you've seen a ghost."

"I have to go to the office," Lissa said. "I have to find out how this letter got here."

"You mean it isn't a note from your mother or something?" Josh asked.

"I can't explain. I'll be fine. You can go back to class now." Lissa was yanking open the office door, desperate for information. Josh didn't answer, but he didn't leave, either.

Lissa rushed to the head secretary, sitting behind the desk in the office, finishing up a phone conversation. "Excuse me," Lissa said, voice shaking.

"Yes?"

"This letter was just sent to me in English class. Can you tell me how it was left?"

The secretary looked at the envelope in Lissa's hand. "Oh yes," she said. "A very attractive man came in with a transcript of your school records from your previous school. Noted at the bottom was your transfer to our school. He wanted to know if you were a student here, and when I said yes, he said it was very important that you get that letter. I hope it wasn't bad news."

"Did you give him any other information?" Lissa asked desperately. "Did you give him my address?"

"Why no, I didn't," the secretary said firmly. "We don't give that out without authorization."

Lissa sighed in relief. That was the first break she'd gotten.

"Oh my," the secretary then said, her hand covering her mouth.

"What?" Lissa asked, more sharply than she meant to.

"You know, he did look at the computer screen when I pulled up your schedule."

"And it had my address?"

"Yes, right there at the top."

Lissa turned on her heel, heading for the door.

"Is there a problem?" the secretary asked.

Lissa didn't even bother to answer. Josh raced along with her as she sprinted out of the building.

"Lissa. Lissa! Where are you going? What's wrong?"

Where was she going? All Lissa knew was that school was no longer safe. She hadn't really thought about where she was going or how she was going to get there. She had to get away. She didn't know how, but she had to run.

Then the realization hit. Bird. She had to get him first. She couldn't run without Bird. It might already be too late.

"Can you take me as far as the end of my road?" Lissa asked Josh. She was desperate to get home, to get to Bird, but she didn't want to involve Josh. It wasn't safe. And it wasn't his problem. The last thing she needed to do was worry about him, too.

"I'll take you home, if that's what you need," Josh said.

"Just to the drive," Lissa insisted. She was grateful that he didn't ask any more questions as they ran to his car and sped off.

Lissa sat in silence as Josh drove, her mind racing. She had to get Bird; that was definitely first. Then what? Where could she go? Where did she have even a chance of being safe?

Maybe she should try to get away with Josh.

No. She couldn't involve him. She didn't know what awaited her, but she knew that Josh didn't deserve to have to deal with it. Once she got Bird, she'd find a way.

"Please let me take you the rest of the way," Josh said. "You're obviously upset, and I don't want to leave you."

"If you care about me at all, you'll leave me here. Trust me, Josh. I know what I'm doing." Lissa tried desperately to make Josh believe that lie.

"Lissa," Josh said, "I'd do anything to help you. You should know that by now."

"Then drop me right here and go back to school. Everything will be fine. There's just somebody I need to see, and I need to do it by myself. I'll see you in school tomorrow."

"Promise?" Josh said, still with a disturbed look on his face.

"Promise," Lissa said, hating to lie to Josh. "Thanks. Goodbye." She got out of the car, waiting until he turned around and slowly left, then setting off at a run down the drive toward the house. Toward Bird.

Nothing seemed different at the house, at least from the outside. There was no car in the front, nobody in evidence. Still, Lissa knew that meant nothing. Hand shaking, she put the key in the lock. Please, she said, over and over in her head. Please let me hear Bird call out when he hears the door open. Please.

She heard nothing but silence. Lissa froze inside the door, but desperation sent her running to her bedroom. Where was Bird? Why wasn't he calling to her?

Her bedroom door was shut. Someone had been there because she always left her door open. Lissa's heart was beating so frantically that she thought it would explode. Somehow, though, she turned the knob, then pushed open the door.

Silence greeted her.

She rushed into the room, crossing to the window where Bird's cage stood. It was empty. Stuck between the bars was another torn piece of paper. She pulled it out, sinking to the floor.

It had the same block writing as the letter she had gotten at school, and it had the same message.

You're dead.

That was all it said. That was all it needed to say.

Chapter 19

Where was Bird? Through the misery that flooded Lissa, that thought surfaced. What was happening to her was bad enough, but had it killed Bird, too? Tears came to her eyes; despair overwhelmed her. Still, though, something else began to surface. She wasn't sure what she was feeling — anger or an instinct for survival or a desire for revenge for Bird's sake. Whatever it was, it galvanized her into action.

She looked out her bedroom windows, searching for signs of motion. She studied each section of the woods, watched, listened. Although she thought the woods seemed quieter than usual, there were still some birds chattering. Maybe nobody was there.

Lissa knew one thing: She could not stay in this house. The thought of being cornered, trapped, was worse than anything the outdoors could hold for her. She looked around quickly, seeing nothing that would help her, nothing she needed except for the fifty dollars that she had stuck inside her dresser drawer the day she had moved into this room.

She opened the door and stepped outside almost with a sense of relief. She had at least the beginning of a plan. She was going to run until she couldn't run any longer down the drive and toward the main road. She would stay off to the side, ready to duck into the trees if she heard a car. Maybe her mother would come back, and she could flag down the car. Maybe she could convince somebody to give her a ride into town. Then she would have to find a place to stay, maybe a hidden place, maybe a public place, until she could contact her mother.

And if that didn't work, she would keep on going, use her money to hire a taxi or rent a room. Beyond that, she couldn't think, couldn't plan.

Lissa had actually taken the first rapid steps toward the drive when a noise stopped her as abruptly as if she had hit an invisible wall. She listened again, filled with a desperate hope that the sound would be repeated. She waited, not breathing, not even blinking her eyes.

There it was again. A smile actually lit up

her face. She knew that sound. There was no mistaking it.

Somewhere in the woods behind the house she heard Bird. He was calling his shrill shriek of complaint, a sound that no wild bird would ever duplicate. Bird was alive, and he was calling to Lissa.

She darted around the house, listening carefully, willing Bird to keep calling to her. The sound was distant, well into the deep part of the woods, audible only because its high pitch let it carry. Lissa had to keep stopping, waiting to hear him before she plunged deeper into the woods, led on by Bird.

At one point he stopped calling, and Lissa panicked. Had something gotten him? She couldn't stand the thought of being so close to rescuing him only to lose him. She whistled to him, thrilled to hear his response, much closer than before. As she made her way further into the woods, shoving aside branches, tripping through the underbrush, Bird called to her more and more frantically, knowing now that she was near. Lissa almost cried when she finally saw him.

Had he not moved, she might not have found him even then. He was on the branch of a pine tree, camouflaged among the needles. As soon as he saw her, he hung upside down by one foot, calling to her joyously. She reached up to him, and he immediately climbed on her finger. She pulled him close to her, talking to him in a whisper.

"Bird, what happened? How did you get here? You couldn't have walked this far, and you couldn't have flown. Are you hurt? I wish you could tell me your story."

Bird stared back at her, tilting his head, blinking his tiny dark eyes. He cooed softly as Lissa stroked his head and held him close, warming him from the chill of the air.

He hadn't gotten there on his own. Lissa stopped to think through that piece of information. Why was Bird this far into the woods? Had he been taken, and then escaped?

Suddenly Lissa heard the footsteps. She had not sensed the presence of anyone else, so occupied had she been with Bird.

Then the second possibility hit her. Had Bird been brought to the woods to lure her here? If so, it had worked perfectly.

She stood motionless. The footsteps had stopped, and her frantic glances could detect no motion, no person. Still, he was there. Of that there could be not doubt.

The voice, when it spoke, startled her so badly that she yelped in surprise. She searched desperately for it, but it was as if the words emanated from the trees with no earthly presence.

"You're dead," the voice said, somewhere between a whisper and a proclamation.

Lissa took off running. She didn't decide, didn't think, didn't weigh her alternatives. She just ran, clutching Bird to her chest, running toward the edge of the woods closest to the house.

She heard no footsteps, no sound of a second person moving through the woods, and she stopped, gasping in ragged gulps of air. She listened. Maybe he was gone. Maybe she could make it either to the house or the road. Suddenly, being in the house seemed better than it had before. She could call the police, barricade the doors, protect the windows. She didn't know how, but at least she could try.

This time, though, the voice came from in front of her, spooking her even more badly than before. How had he gotten there? Why hadn't she seen him?

"I can't kill you. You're already dead," the voice said harshly, chilling Lissa to the bone.

Lissa turned back into the woods, not even trying to move quietly. She wanted distance between herself and the voice. When she could run no further, when the burning muscles in her legs could not move her another step, she ducked behind the biggest tree she could find, leaning against the trunk, willing her breathing to quiet.

This time she saw the glint of the barrel of a rifle of some sort before she heard the voice. She ran again.

Twice more she set off in desperate attempts to escape the voice, but it didn't work. Each time she stopped, the voice greeted her. Finally, she knew that she couldn't run any further. She was cut and bruised from the underbrush and branches she had crashed through, and her lungs and legs had been pushed further than they would endure.

That was when she found the hollowed-out place at the base of the tree and huddled into it, pulling as many leaves as she could over her in a rough covering. That was when she tucked Bird against her throat, and listened for the footsteps to return, and waited for the voice to speak those horrible words.

That was when Lissa waited to die. He would find her. He seemed to have an almost magical ability to move through the woods. And when he found her, he would kill her.

She couldn't think of any way to avoid it. She was out of answers.

As minutes passed, then more, then more, Lissa began, against her better judgment, to hope. Maybe he had given up. Maybe he had just wanted to scare her and didn't really mean to kill her.

Then she heard the footsteps again, quietly moving closer and then away, sweeping over each section. He had lost her temporarily, but he was narrowing down the possibilities, search area by search area.

That was when she began to go back through her memories. She knew that her hiding place was not good enough. She knew that he would kill her. She wondered if anybody would ever know what had happened to her, or if it would be as if she had just disappeared forever.

Did it really matter?

The footsteps came closer, and Bird began to get restless. This is almost over, Lissa thought. A part of her was almost relieved when Bird scrambled out of her hand and gave a loud cry of complaint. The footsteps came more rapidly this time, noisier, rougher.

Then there was another Bird cry. Except it wasn't Bird. It came from Lissa's left at quite a distance. She listened in amazement, totally confused. There simply was no mistaking Bird's cry for any other animal's. Unless there was another gray-cheeked parrot in the woods, which made absolutely no sense, there was no explanation. She listened as the footsteps headed toward the direction of the second cry.

Bird continued to move about, and she was afraid that he would call out again. She grabbed him, pushing him firmly against her stomach. He squirmed and even bit her finger, but she held on to him, muffling his protests.

She heard Bird cry again, still further to the left, carrying faintly through the woods. She couldn't hear the footsteps any longer. She slowly, quietly, raised herself out of the nest at the base of the tree until she was sitting; then she got her legs under her so she was crouching. She listened carefully, hearing nothing.

"Lissa." The voice was behind her, hissed and frantic. "Lissa!" She sank back down, ready to burrow back into the nest. "Princess Lissa!"

Princess Lissa? Only one person in her life had ever called her that.

"Come on. This way," Josh's voice whispered. She looked behind her, not even daring to hope that this wasn't yet another trick to get her where her killer wanted her to be.

Josh's face, grim and tense, peeked out from behind a tree about ten yards away. He held out his hand to her.

She got to her feet, feeling the pain of re-circulating blood.

"Hurry," Josh said, and she cautiously moved toward him. Was this safe? Was she being led into even more danger?

Still, how could it get any worse?

"Follow me," Josh said, locking his gaze onto hers. "We don't have much time."

Lissa followed as he weaved around trees and through the brush almost as if there were a path that he could see although she couldn't. When they reached the edge of the woods nearest the house, he hesitated, then leaned back to whisper to her. "My car is down the drive around the first curve, pulled off to the side. Hurry. We don't have as much cover here."

Lissa followed him as quickly and as quietly as she could, oblivious to the pain. At any second she expected to hear the crack of a gunshot.

Lissa had never in her life been so glad to see a vehicle as she was to see Josh's car. He threw open the door for her, then sprinted to the driver's side. Lissa curled into the passenger's side, holding her breath until the engine roared to life and Josh backed onto the road, then jolted the car forward. He drove down the drive and onto the road that led out of the woods and into town as if all the demons in hell were after them.

Lissa held on until several miles had passed. Then she started to shake, and tears spilled down her face silently. Josh, still driving fast, reached one hand over and touched the tears.

"How did you know?" she finally asked, her voice hoarse.

"I started driving back to school after I dropped you off, arguing with myself all the way. One part of me said that I should respect your wishes, and the other part said that something wasn't right and I should check it out."

"So you came back?"

"My cousins and I used to play in those woods all the time when we were kids, especially after the lodge burned down. I figured I could circle around the house through the woods, check to see that you were all right, and leave without your ever knowing that I was there."

Lissa turned to look behind them. No car was in sight.

"But then weird things were happening. I saw a man in the woods, carrying a bird that was screaming at the top of its lungs. I heard the man curse when the bird bit him."

Lissa smiled down at Bird.

"Then I saw him put the bird in the tree.

Once I could see him, I knew it had to be your bird from the way you described him. I couldn't figure out what was going on, so I went further into the woods to stay out of his way and watch."

"Then I came?"

"Yeah, and that's when things got really crazy. Lissa, that man had a gun, and he was stalking you."

"I know," Lissa said.

"I couldn't figure out how to get him away from you, and I was almost ready to just rush him and try to get the gun when you disappeared."

"I hid at the base of a tree," Lissa said.

"Good plan," Josh responded. "That gave me a chance to get to his other side, and when Bird called, I imitated him to draw the man away from you."

"You sounded just like Bird," Lissa said.

"That's my grandmother again," Josh said with a smile. "She's had me imitating the calls of the birds that feed in her yard since I was a little kid. I do a great cardinal, and a passable blue jay. My best is a tufted titmouse."

"I hate to think what could have happened," Lissa said with a shudder. "He could have killed you."

"He was much more interested in you," Josh

said, his voice getting very serious. "Lissa, who was that man? Why was he after you?"

Lissa paused for a long moment.

"Is he some stranger who's been stalking you? The newspaper had a story about that just the other day."

Lissa shook her head no.

"It's not an old boyfriend or something like that, is it? He looked too old for that."

"Not a boyfriend," Lissa said, her voice barely audible.

"Then who is it, Lissa? Who was in that woods trying to kill you?"

Tears streamed down Lissa's face. Josh deserved an answer, but she couldn't say the words.

Chapter 20

Josh took Lissa and Bird straight to his grandmother. She greeted Lissa warmly and immediately convinced Bird to get onto her
finger, after which the two communed like old
friends. Josh, however, quickly interrupted to
tell his grandmother what he knew of what had
happened in the woods. Lissa could barely
make herself speak. Now that she was behind
the closed doors of an environment that
seemed safe, she felt herself get shakier and
shakier.

Josh's grandmother listened in astonishment, then immediately reached for the phone.
"I'm calling the police," she said firmly.

"No," Lissa said quickly. After all, that
wasn't the way it worked. Nobody told family
secrets.

"Lissa, unless there's something I'm miss-
ing, a man tried to kill you. He has a gun. If

he isn't still a danger to you, he's a danger to other people. Or to himself," she added seriously.

Lissa had never thought of that. She had always assumed that she was the only problem. She sat motionless as the phone call was made, dreading the need to tell the story again to strangers who might not even believe her. After all, it did sound crazy, paranoid.

"Don't worry, Lissa. I'll be right here. I'll help you tell them," Josh said, almost as if he could read her mind.

That helped some, but she still shook, flashing back to the terror in the woods, not wanting to relive it in words. Josh's grandmother jolted her into action, sending Josh to the garage for a pruning saw, then taking Lissa into the yard to find branches for Bird. Together they cut four or five, then anchored them on a block of wood, providing a variety of perches for Bird. Next they went to the kitchen where they found an apple and some grapes, which Bird tasted before climbing around on the branches, choosing one, and settling down to nap. He'd had quite a day so far, Lissa thought.

Of course, so had she. It was hard to imagine that only hours ago she had been sitting in English class, pretending to lead a normal life.

While waiting for the police to arrive, Lissa

tried to get in touch with her mother. There was no answer at either house so she left messages on both answering machines, giving Josh's grandmother's phone number and telling her to call immediately. Beyond that, she didn't explain. What kind of message could she leave?

Telling the story to the police was even worse than she had imagined. There were two of them, both men, and they asked questions she didn't want to answer.

"Tell the truth, Lissa," Josh's grandmother prompted her gently. "None of this is your fault. You have nothing to hide."

Lissa left out a lot of the detail, but she told them most of it. The policemen quickly said that they were going out to the house in the woods, and that she should stay where she was until the man who had tried to kill her was apprehended.

Apprehended. That made him sound like a criminal.

"He tried to kill you, Lissa," Josh's grandmother said after the policemen were gone. "He needs help."

Lissa nodded, tears filling her eyes.

"Come here," Josh's grandmother said, going to sit on the sofa beside Lissa and putting her arms around her. Lissa held herself rigidly away, uncomfortable with the contact. "Why don't you rest for a little bit? You're about ready to fall over, all that running and hiding. Come with me." She led Lissa to a second floor bedroom. The ceiling sloped down from a center peak, and a single bed covered with a brightly patterned quilt was next to the window. A framed print of pansies and daisies decorated one wall.

Lissa lay on the bed, amazed at how good it felt to put her head down. Then she heard Bird call out and immediately sat up again.

"I'll take care of him," Josh's grandmother said. "You just try to relax a little."

Josh followed his grandmother out of the room, his eyes gentle. Lissa curled into a ball, her arms around her knees, and shut her eyes. Over and over again she heard the whispered words: *I can't kill you. You're already dead.*

She must have dozed off briefly because at first she couldn't place the ringing of the telephone. She heard the murmur of Josh's grandmother's voice, then footsteps coming to her room. "Your mother's on her way."

Lissa opened her eyes and nodded, then closed her eyes again. She didn't know how she felt about that. She loved her mother, that was a given, but she also felt that her mother was a little bit responsible for this.

She lay on the bed, pretending to be asleep, until she heard her mother's arrival. She let Josh and his grandmother fill her in. Lissa heard her mother's footsteps on the stairs, then felt her burst into the room and sit on the bed next to Lissa, stroking her hair.

"Lissa, I'm so sorry. I thought you were safe."

"I know," Lissa said, almost too softly to be heard. The phone rang downstairs again, and then Josh's grandmother came up.

"Mrs. Davis, they need you at the police station."

"Do you want to go with me?" her mother asked.

"No," Lissa said without hesitation.

"Could she possibly wait here?" her mother asked Josh's grandmother. "I know we're imposing on your good will."

"Nonsense," Josh's grandmother interrupted. "Leave Lissa here with me."

"Thank you," Lissa said, wondering why she was being so kind to a stranger who had put her grandson at risk. Josh circled in and out, anxious to help but not knowing what to do.

The rest of that day, through the night, and into the next day was a blur of phone calls and visits from the police. By the time it was done,

Lissa was ready to scream every time the phone or doorbell rang. She apologized over and over again to Josh's grandmother.

"Lissa honey, don't apologize to me," she said, by this time having invited Lissa to call her Gran. "This is the most excitement I've had in my life in years. It's just like being in the middle of one of those novels by John Grisham."

More like a horror story by Stephen King, Lissa though. She was boundlessly grateful to both Josh and Gran, her links to some kind of sanity.

She almost panicked when her mother came back to Gran's house. "Thank you," she said. "We've caused far too much uproar in your life. I'll take Lissa with me now."

"Let her stay here until things get settled. She's safe here with me," Gran said.

"I couldn't possibly . . ." Lissa's mother began.

"Why don't you ask Lissa what she wants," Gran said.

"I want to stay here," Lissa said. Josh smiled broadly at her. She couldn't summon up a smile in response, but she appreciated his enthusiasm.

She refused to go back to the house, not wanting any part of the woods again, so Josh and her mother went and got her belongings and Bird's cage.

"I'll be back as soon as I căn," her mother said, hugging Lissa fiercely.

"It's okay," Lissa said, and she partly meant it.

Chapter 21

It took months, but finally Lissa got answers. Horrifying as they were, they helped. For the first time, she understood.

Vietnam, it turned out, was the reason behind it all.

During the last week of Lissa's father's tour of duty in Vietnam, he and eleven other soldiers had been sent to check a tiny village that supposedly had armed communist supporters. Two soldiers from their company had been killed the day before by snipers, and more snipers were rumored to be everywhere. The soldiers, tense and unnerved by the deaths of their buddies, burst into the village, guns ready. Ten or twelve people had already been rounded up when a figure emerged from one of the huts, holding a cylindrical object pointed toward Lissa's father. He fired before the person could fire at him, thinking that he was facing a gun.

It was only after a woman broke loose from the group being held and threw herself on the body, crying as she cradled it, that Lissa's father realized what he had done. The person he had shot was a young girl of about sixteen. What she had been holding out was a rolled piece of paper on which she had drawn a beautifully detailed sketch of a green bird. The sobbing woman unfurled the paper and shoved it at Lissa's father, finally throwing it at his feet. Then the woman returned to the body, stroking the long dark hair of the dead girl.

The psychiatrists at the hospital called it a severe case of post-traumatic stress disorder. There were certain things about Lissa that triggered memories of the horror of what her father had done in Vietnam. Her long, dark hair had been perhaps one of the first, and as she approached the same age as the girl he had killed, the identification had become even more intense. The final push into madness had been, inadvertently, the eerie parallel of Lissa and the green bird. Something in her father had snapped then, and he had lost touch with any reality other than his acting out of the buried trauma. The only reason it hadn't been worse earlier, the psychiatrists thought, was because his art was a subconscious release. The violent reds and oranges and slashing lines were his way of releasing the pain and fear and blood and death of the war.

But even that hadn't been enough so he had tried to kill his own daughter. Only it wasn't really Lissa that he hunted. It was the ghost of the girl he had killed in Vietnam, a ghost that was already dead but wouldn't stop haunting him.

"I can't kill you. You're already dead." Those words now made some sense to Lissa when they echoed in her waking nightmares.

And yet, despite it all, she felt sympathy for her father. He had been a young man who went into the Army to escape a father he hated, and he ended up in a war that he hated even more.

The doctors believed that with a lot of time and therapy, and with the support of other Vietnam vets who had lived through their own horror stories in the war, Lissa's father would recover. He would have to endure the pain of confronting his past and making some kind of peace with it. Never again could it fester unacknowledged, poisoning whatever he touched.

Never again could he be a desperate man

in the woods with a gun, trying to kill a daughter who had only tried to earn his love. Lissa was alive, and never again could he think she was the young girl who had died holding out a picture of a small green bird to a frightened soldier. He would have to put this behind him now, just as Lissa had to put her past behind her.

An arrangement was finally made concerning Lissa. She would live with Gran and finish her senior year, figuring out college along the way. Gran insisted that Lissa was a joy to have, and she absolutely doted on Bird. After a week or so when Lissa returned to school, Bird didn't even call out after her since he was already sitting on Gran's shoulder getting ready to go out and play in a tree while she raked leaves.

Lissa missed her mother at times, but there was a distance between them that was not yet bridged. That would take time and healing, too.

And then there was Josh. Gran had to force him to go home to his parents. If he had his way, he would have stayed with them permanently, but Gran wouldn't hear of it. "Lissa needs some space, so back off and let her breathe. Besides, I've only had a grandson, and now I have a granddaughter. This is now the women's domain. Men can only visit when we let them."

Lissa and Gran baked bread and raked leaves and sometimes, late at night, talked about the really hard stuff. Tiny bit by tiny bit, Lissa felt some of the fear and anger and sorrow leave until she could once again laugh at Bird and talk about her father without crying.

Josh, with infinite patience, kept trying to cheer her up. He took her for walks, drove her to school, bought her chocolate chip ice cream, and even convinced her, one brisk evening heading into winter, to go to the movies with him.

"You'll learn to trust me," he told her, flashing that grin.

"How?" Lissa asked, despairing that she would ever be able to simply believe the best about a person.

"I'll never do anything to let you down," he said. "Day after day, I'll be honest with you, and I'll never intentionally hurt you. After about seven thousand and eight days of this, you'll begin to realize that this is something you can count on — that I'm someone you can count on."

Lissa smiled. "Seven thousand and eight?" she asked.

"That's always been my lucky number," Josh said with a smile. He reached over and took Lissa's hand in his, twining his fingers with hers.

Lissa didn't pull her hand away.

Point Horror

Dare you read

NIGHTMARE HALL

Where college is a
scream!

High on a hill overlooking Salem University hidden in shadows and shrouded in mystery, sits Nightingale Hall.

Nightmare Hall, the students call it. Because that's where the terror began...

Don't miss these spine-tingling thrillers:

The Silent Scream	*Pretty Please*
The Roommate	*The Experiment*
Deadly Attraction	*The Nightwalker*
The Wish	*Sorority Sister*
The Scream Team	*Last Date*
Guilty	